As an evil traitor threatens to destroy
the top-secret SPEAR agency,
A YEAR OF LOVING DANGEROUSLY
continues....

Margarita Alfonsa de las Fuentes
Beautiful and utterly bewitching—
her heart is held captive by only one man.

*The fiery spy lives by her own set of rules.
She does what she wants...when she wants!
Except now her hot-blooded lover's scorching
kisses threaten to shatter her self-control...
and blow her cover.*

Carlos Caballero
His smoldering black eyes and disarming smile
make all the women swoon.

*Whether Margarita wants his protection or not,
this lean, bronzed warrior is not going to let a
deadly felon harm one hair on her head.
For he will risk it all for the beguiling woman
he is determined to possess!*

Marcus Waters
Dashing and charismatic,
he is a thorn in Caballero's side.

*Either the heat of the Central American jungle is
getting to him...or Agent Waters really does
harbor a secret desire. But there will be hell to
pay if his dark-tempered rival ever catches on!*

Dear Reader,

It's the beginning of a new year, and Intimate Moments is ready to kick things off with six more fabulously exciting novels. Readers have been clamoring for Linda Turner to create each new installment of her wonderful miniseries THOSE MARRYING McBRIDES! In *Never Been Kissed* she honors those wishes with the deeply satisfying tale of virginal nurse Janey McBride and Dr. Reilly Jones, who's just the man to teach her how wonderful love can be when you share it with the right man.

A YEAR OF LOVING DANGEROUSLY continues to keep readers on the edge of their seats with *The Spy Who Loved Him,* bestselling author Merline Lovelace's foray into the dangerous jungles of Central America, where the loving is as steamy as the air. And you won't want to miss *My Secret Valentine,* the enthralling conclusion to our in-line 36 HOURS spin-off. As always, Marilyn Pappano delivers a page-turner you won't be able to resist. Ruth Langan begins a new trilogy, THE SULLIVAN SISTERS, with *Awakening Alex,* sure to be another bestseller. Lyn Stone's second book for the line, *Live-In Lover,* is sure to make you her fan. Finally, welcome brand-new New Zealand sensation Frances Housden. In *The Man for Maggie* she makes a memorable debut, one that will have you crossing your fingers that her next book will be out soon.

Enjoy! And come back next month, when the excitement continues here in Silhouette Intimate Moments.

Yours,

Leslie J. Wainger
Executive Senior Editor

Please address questions and book requests to:
Silhouette Reader Service
U.S.: 3010 Walden Ave., P.O. Box 1325, Buffalo, NY 14269
Canadian: P.O. Box 609, Fort Erie, Ont. L2A 5X3

Merline Lovelace
The Spy Who Loved Him

INTIMATE MOMENTS™

Published by Silhouette Books

America's Publisher of Contemporary Romance

Special thanks and acknowledgment are given to
Merline Lovelace for her contribution to the
A Year of Loving Dangerously series.

To the one, the only Al, mi amigo, mi amor, mi esposo

 SILHOUETTE BOOKS

ISBN 0-373-27122-0

THE SPY WHO LOVED HIM

Visit Silhouette at www.eHarlequin.com

Printed in U.S.A.

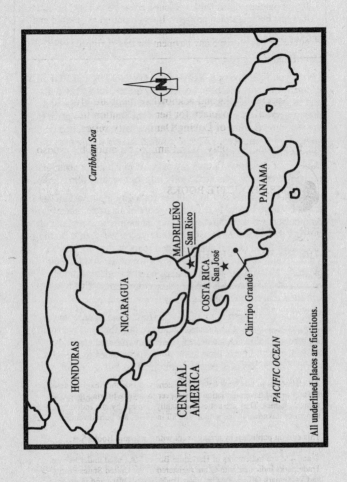

All underlined places are fictitious.

A note from reader favorite Merline Lovelace,
author of over fifteen unforgettable novels for Silhouette Books:

Dear Reader,

I hope you're enjoying A YEAR OF LOVING DANGEROUSLY
as much as I am! I've been holding my breath, biting my nails
and heaving huge sighs of relief with each narrow escape and
dreamy, romantic ending. This slice of the action takes place in
the steaming jungles of Madrileño, a tiny country perched on the
edge of the Caribbean. I have to confess the sexy, supermacho
hero—a colonel in the Madrileñan army serving as the deputy
minister of defense—flutters my pulse as much as he does that
of the secret agent who stubbornly refuses to marry him.

Okay, okay! I admit it. I'm a sucker for a guy in uniform. I guess
that's because I spent twenty-three years in air force blue myself.
And because of a certain sexy young captain who swept me off
my feet three decades ago. Over those years, we shared exciting,
adventure-filled careers that included tours of duty in Taiwan,
Vietnam and at the Pentagon in the Office of the Joint Chiefs
of Staff. We even got to pin on each other's eagles. Although
Al occasionally reminds me he made colonel first, I've never
admitted that he outranks me.

Now that we've both hung up our uniforms, we're enjoying golf,
long, lazy dinners with friends and traveling. Last fall we spent
the most delicious two weeks in Germany, Austria and Italy.
Hong Kong and Paris used to be my favorite cities in the whole
world. Venice has now edged them out. This fall we're off
to…wherever the winds take us.

With that kind of romance and adventure in my blood, it's no
surprise that characters like Margarita and Carlos steal my heart.
Here's hoping they capture yours, too!

And if you enjoyed this book, watch for my next. *The Horse
Soldier* features another military hero—the leather-tough
commander of a cavalry regiment stationed on Wyoming's wild,
untamed frontier. A January 2001 release from MIRA Books,
The Horse Soldier is available now.

Merline Lovelace

Chapter 1

"Why doesn't he marry *her!* The way she drapes herself all over him, any fool can see Anna would love Carlos to wrap her in silver gauze and shield her from every cold breeze that blows her way."

Muttering into her crystal champagne flute, Margarita Alfonsa de las Fuentes leaned silk-sheathed hips against a stone balustrade. Behind her, the city of San Rico, capital of Madrileño, spilled down steep, jungle-covered slopes to a sea awash in moonlight. In front of her, tall French doors thrown open to the balmy January night gave an unobstructed view of the glittering crowd gathered to

welcome the new Austrian ambassador to Madrileño. Dancers in flowing gowns and elegant tuxe-
dos swirled and dipped across the State Ballroom's
shining parquet floor to the lively strains of the
"Blue Danube Waltz."

One dancer in particular held Margarita's attention. Her cousin, Anna. Tiny, beautiful Anna, with
the melting brown eyes, thick black lashes and
tumbling masses of the blue-black hair most Madrileñans were blessed with. Slender as the swaying
sugarcane plants that formed the basis of their
country's economy, Anna moved with a feather-
light grace that thoroughly annoyed her cousin. As
Margarita knew all too well, delicate, seemingly
fragile Anna possessed the face of an angel and the
temper of a wasp. The twenty-year-old could make
life miserable for everyone around her when things
didn't go her way.

Not that her dancing partner would care about
her temper. Or even notice it. If Carlos married
Anna, he'd spoil her outrageously…then leave her
to sit docile and pampered at home while he went
about the important business of men. He wouldn't
be around enough to notice her vile moods, which
in any case Anna would hide from him like a
proper little wife.

But Carlos didn't want to marry Anna. He'd decided on Margarita as his bride-to-be. He'd even obtained her father's consent to the match.

Gritting her teeth against an all too familiar frustration, she tossed her head and downed the last of her champagne. Even now, three years after returning from an extended stay in the States, she still battled the chauvinism that permeated every social stratum in her country. Each time she made a small dent in the masculine dominance—as when she'd landed her job at the Ministry of Economics over her father's vehement objections—she'd stumble up against another obstacle.

Like Carlos.

Carlos Caballero. Madrileño's Deputy Minister of Defense. Six feet plus of solid muscle, bronzed skin, glossy black hair and calm self-confidence. Margarita had known him most of her life and had adamantly refused to marry him for the past year...despite her mother's fervent urging, her father's blustery demands and the traitorous needles of desire that shot through her whenever Carlos turned his sexy onyx eyes in her direction.

The fact that he sprang from the same aristocratic roots she did, had racked up a chest full of medals during his military service and was considered the brightest mind in the Ministry of Defense didn't overcome the man's liabilities as a life partner in Margarita's mind. He was everything she didn't want in a husband. Conservative. Traditional. Overprotective.

It didn't matter that he also possessed a smile that made girls sigh and grown women walk into walls. Or that he moved with a pantherlike grace under his elegantly tailored tuxedo. Or even that Margarita's chest tightened whenever she imagined his lean, muscled body pinning her to the sheets.

What mattered was that he shared the oppressive, antiquated view of marriage of so many Madrileñan men. She'd broken with her family once over their clamoring desire that she marry someone of their choosing. Fled to the United States for six years of college and graduate school. Gotten involved with an organization that would shock her parents to their core if they knew about it.

She'd come back to Madrileño three years ago. She would always come back to Madrileño. Her country was in her blood, a part of her heritage.

Sighing, Margarita set aside the crystal flute and turned to lean her elbows on the stone balustrade. As it always did, the spectacular collage of dark, jungle-covered mountains, white-washed buildings topped with red tile roofs and shimmering sea grabbed at her heart. The city of San Rico combined everything she loved and hated about her country…breathtaking beauty surrounded by feral wilderness; fabulous wealth wrenched from abject poverty; a cosmopolitan elite leading a population still struggling with illiteracy and centuries of oppression.

She was determined to help her country rise to the promise of the new millennium. Determined as well to eradicate the drug trade that had crippled its economy for years. That's why she'd fought for her job with the Ministry of Economics. Why she'd joined SPEAR when she was approached as a graduate student at the University of Pennsylvania. Why she…

"You look especially beautiful in moonlight."

The deep, chocolate-smooth voice raised goose bumps on Margarita's bare shoulders and arms. She turned, and the sight of Carlos in white tie and black tux raised goose bumps everywhere else.

How did he do it? she wondered irritably. How could he look so devilishly handsome and so maddeningly complacent at the same time? And how did he manage to set her back up with a mere compliment? She wasn't idiotic enough to wish he admired her for her mind *instead* of her looks, but an occasional acknowledgment of her intellect might have elevated his standing in her eyes considerably.

"Thank you."

Her terse response lifted one of his brows. Strolling across the balcony, he joined her at the railing. At five-seven, Margarita was considered tall for a Madrileñan. Even so, she had to tilt her head to look into Carlos's chiseled features.

"I like you in red," he murmured. His gaze drifted down her throat to the swell of her breasts. "What there is of it."

"I'm so glad." Oozing syrupy sweetness, she smoothed her palms over the flame-colored sheath that plunged to a deep V in both front and back. "I thought of you when I chose this gown."

A corner of his mouth turned up. "I'm sure you did. You take particular delight in taunting me, do you not, *querida?*"

The lazy half smile caused a distinct flutter in Margarita's chest. As much as she'd like to, she couldn't deny the man's impact on her central nervous system. Carlos radiated masculinity. Smooth, controlled, extremely potent masculinity. Ignoring the treacherous skip in her pulse, she took issue with his casual endearment.

"I don't suppose it would do any good to remind you that I am not now, nor will I ever be, your 'darling'?"

"No good at all," he replied easily. "Any more than it would do for me to remind you that 'ever' is a long time. I'm a patient man. Very patient."

"Yes, I know."

For some reason, the patience he took such pride

in irritated Margarita more than anything else. If ever a man didn't fit the English translation of his last name...

Steady, sober Carlos Caballero was as far from a cowboy as she'd come across in her thirty years. She'd never seen him lose his temper. Never witnessed a single crack in his iron discipline. She wanted passion from the man she married. Mindless, senseless, damn-the-consequences passion.

"You're wasting your time, Carlos. I've told you repeatedly, I won't marry someone who intends to shield his wife from everything nasty life has to offer."

"It's a man's nature to want to protect his woman."

Before she could take umbrage with that Neanderthal bit of philosophy, his wide shoulders lifted in a shrug.

"I can't change who I am, Rita, any more than you can change who you are."

"You don't have the faintest idea of who I am," she countered flatly.

None of them did. Her parents. Her friends. Her waspish little cousin Anna. Not one of them even faintly suspected that Margarita had been recruited by SPEAR while attending school in the States.

SPEAR—the acronym succinctly summed up its mission: Stealth, Perseverance, Endeavor, Attack and Rescue. The Washington, D.C. based organization was so secret that few members of the U.S. government and even fewer in the international community knew of its existence. Yet its tentacles reached deeply into domestic and foreign affairs, as well as into the business sector.

Although Margarita had undergone the same brutal training as SPEAR's other agents, she'd been recruited for a specific mission and sent home right after her training. For three years, she'd quietly fed information on the Latin American drug trade to SPEAR. She took fierce pride in the fact that her efforts cut deeply into the illegal traffic that had almost destroyed her country's economy.

"I know all I need to know about you, *querida*," Carlos said quietly, pulling her attention to the discussion at hand. "We'd make a good match."

"Why?" Her chin came up. "Because my uncle is the President of Madrileño and he wants you to run for the senate seat that's just come open?"

She wasn't sure, but she thought she caught a flicker of annoyance in his eyes. She felt a dart of triumph at having pierced his impenetrable calm, even for a second. The feeling evaporated when he moved closer. Only a step or two, just enough to crowd Margarita against the stone railing behind her.

"If I sought a wife for merely political purposes, I'd choose someone far more malleable."

"Like Anna?" she inquired sweetly, all too aware of the heady combination of starched shirt and tangy aftershave she drew in with every breath.

"Like Anna," he agreed. "But it's you I want, Margarita."

"Why?" she demanded again, annoyed anew by his stubborn refusal to accept defeat. "Why do you insist on pursuing a woman who doesn't want you?"

The smile came back into his eyes. "Maybe because she's yet to make me believe she doesn't."

"Madre di Dios!" Thoroughly exasperated, she shook her head. "Just what does it take to convince you?"

"I don't know. Shall we put it to the test?"

Planting his hands on the railing on either side of her, Carlos leaned forward. Margarita understood his intent well before his mouth brushed hers. She could have stopped him with an icy command. Could have jerked her head away, or even taken him down with one of the many maneuvers she'd learned during SPEAR's rigorous defensive countermeasures training. Instead, she kept her face impassive and her mouth tilted to his. What better way to demonstrate how unsuited they were than to let him see how little his kisses affected her?

She might have convinced both him and herself if he'd stopped after the first soft brush of his lips on hers. Unfortunately for her peace of mind, he didn't. With a smooth coordination, he slid an arm around her waist and drew her close. She felt him against every inch of her body, as hard as tempered steel. His mouth came down on hers, more firmly this time, with a sensual deliberation that infuriated Margarita even as it set off tiny detonations under her skin.

Warmth flowed into her veins. Desire fisted in her belly. She could feel the studs in his shirt through the thin silk of her gown. Feel, too, the ripple of muscle in the arm locked around her waist. For an insane moment, she reveled in his strength and in the heat shooting through her. Only the fact that he'd stoked the fire so deliberately kept her from flinging her arms around his neck and consigning herself to the flames.

To her profound disgust, her whole body trembled when at last he raised his head. She drew in a shaky breath and was just preparing to let loose with both barrels when another sensation penetrated her whirling senses.

A slow vibration against her bare skin.

Just above her breasts.

Her hand flew to the wafer-thin locket she wore on a gold chain around her neck. The modest piece of jewelry didn't go with her designer gown, which called for diamonds or flashy rubies, but Margarita never went anywhere without the small, oblong gold disk. When she flattened a palm over the locket and felt its barely discernible signal, excitement shoved everything but one thought from her mind.

SPEAR. She had to find a private corner, and fast! Someplace she could use the tiny transceiver tucked in her beaded handbag. With a toss of her head, she cut Carlos off at the knees.

"That was…enjoyable. Now if you'll excuse me, I'd better return to the ball."

Enjoyable!

Carlos waited until she'd swept through the open French doors to unclench the fists he'd dug into his pockets.

There was nothing the least enjoyable about that kiss! Every nerve in his body snapped with desire. His groin ached so fiercely, he could barely stand upright. Another moment or two with Margarita's mouth under his and he would have dragged her down on the damned balcony, ripped off that handkerchief she called a gown and blown his chances with her forever.

He knew her so well. He'd watched her mature from a bright, eager girl into a stubborn, determined woman. Had wanted her for as long as he could remember. He'd been biding his time since she returned from the States, waiting for her to find a middle ground between the liberal concepts she'd absorbed during her years abroad and the more traditional ways of Madrileño. He'd declared himself a year ago and waited patiently for her to recognize how well matched they were. At this moment, he wasn't sure he was going to survive the wait!

Intellectually, Carlos accepted that Margarita had to find her own way to him. That he couldn't force her into his bed…as much as he'd like to. Nor could he force her to admit she wasn't any more immune to the electricity that crackled between them than he was. All he could do was keep applying pressure. And keep in rigid check his growing urge to claim her in the most elemental way a man can claim his woman.

Holding back got more and more difficult every day. At the thought of her thick, silky black hair tumbling over naked shoulders and her slender body hot and urgent beneath his, the ache in his groin doubled.

Shaking his head at the follies of men, Carlos reached into his tuxedo pocket for a cigar. From past encounters with the stubborn woman he was determined to make his own, he knew it would take some time before the clamor in his body subsided and he could rejoin the others in the ballroom.

A wry smile twisting his lips, he bit off the end of the cigar. Margarita had no idea the knots she tied in his gut with a single flash of her magnificent violet eyes. If he was to retain any semblance of his masculinity, Carlos had better make sure she never did.

The way he felt right now, that might be far easier said than done.

Impatience beat at Margarita like the wings of the millions of monarch butterflies that made Madrileño their summer home. Dodging guests with a smile and the excuse that she was looking for her father, she slipped down one brilliantly lit corridor after another. It was almost impossible to find a private niche in the Presidential Palace that served double duty as the seat of government as well as her aunt and uncle's home. Ball guests mingled in the anterooms and hallways, exchanging news about the latest diplomatic crises. Uniformed aides hurried to and fro. Servants jumped to open doors.

Finally she found a deserted chamber. The small room with its deep crimson walls and gilt-edged

portraits of past presidents was used to receive
lesser diplomats. Its single door and heavy velvet
drapes that would absorb sound suited her needs
perfectly.

Closing the door behind her, she fumbled in her
beaded bag for a small, flat instrument closely re-
sembling an ordinary cellular phone. Only she and
the other SPEAR operatives knew the powerful ca-
pabilities packed into its innocuous plastic case.
She punched in her code, spoke a few casual words
and waited for the voice-activated sensors at the
other end to verify her identity.

When she was patched into Central Control, she
recognized the agent who responded immediately.
Rangy, blue-eyed Marcus Waters had shared
weeks of brutal survival training with Margarita—
and let her know in his grinning, cocky way that
he wouldn't mind sharing a bed with her as well.
She'd laughed off his offer at the time, but she
wasn't laughing as she listened to the astounding
information Marcus relayed.

"We just got word your Madrileñan police
bagged a very interesting fish in that big drug bust
yesterday."

"Who?" she demanded, too keyed up after her
session with Carlos for word games.

"Brace yourself, babe. From the physical description flashed over the Net, we think he may be Simon.''

Margarita's jaw dropped. "The man we've been hunting the past six months? The same man we suspect of executing a personal vendetta against SPEAR?''

"That's the one," Marcus said cheerfully. "Jonah's in the air as we speak, on his way to San Rico.''

Jonah! The shadowy head of SPEAR. He was legend in the agency. A voice on the phone. A cryptic telegram. A cassette tape hand-delivered in a bouquet of flowers. The fact that he was now enroute to San Rico set her pulse jumping.

"He wants you to hightail it over to the Bastille where your guys are holding Simon," Marcus instructed. "Just to make sure the bastard doesn't bribe his way out of custody.''

In the midst of her clamoring excitement, Margarita could still feel a twinge of pique on behalf of her countrymen. "Not every Latin American official takes bribes.''

"Of course not. Only the ones who've gone bad. And unfortunately, they aren't restricted to Latin American. Let me know as soon as you get Simon in your gun sights.''

"Will do.''

Her momentary irritation forgotten, Margarita

jammed the transmitter into her purse and willed herself to walk sedately through the crowded corridors. At last she reached the tall, arched doors that led to the plaza outside. Weaving her way through the limos lining the square, she quickly plotted her course of action.

Her condo was less than a block away, one of a cluster of new buildings that clung to a steep hillside. She'd purchased the airy little one-bedroom over her father's strenuous objections and her mother's very vocal fears for a young girl living alone. It hadn't done the least good for Margarita to remind her mother she'd left girlhood behind her years ago.

She could change and arrive at the grim fortress that served as Madrileño's central prison in less than ten minutes. Fifteen at most. From past visits to the dark, dank prison, she knew the rats that scurried along its narrow passages were the size of small dogs. She wasn't going inside its walls until she donned a long-sleeved blouse, sturdy jeans and boots.

She wouldn't need to invent an excuse to see the prisoner. As the niece of the President, she could pretty well go where she wished. Just in case anyone asked, though, she'd fabricate a cover story about needing to interview the prisoner to gather information for her job as an analyst at the Ministry of Economics.

In her simmering excitement, Margarita didn't so much as glance over her shoulder at the ornate facade of the Presidential Palace...or spare a thought for the man she'd left cooling his heels on its balcony.

A relic of the days of Spanish rule, the Castillo San Giorgo sat like a stone monolith on a spit of land jutting into the sea. Almost five feet thick at the base, its walls had been constructed of a local stone the conquistadores had labeled coquina. The Spanish had used the same material to construct their fort at Saint Augustine, Florida, which Margarita had visited during her years in the States.

In English, coquina meant little shells, which was precisely what the stone consisted of—millions of tiny shellfish that had died eons ago. Their shells had bonded over time to form an almost indestructible stone embedded with tiny, razorlike bits of shell.

After checking her purse with its little radio and her snub-nosed .38 at the entry to avoid setting off the metal detectors, Margarita was careful not to brush against the walls as she followed the captain of the prison through dank, dark corridors. Not long ago, political prisoners had been crammed into the subterranean rooms the Spanish had once used for storing powder and supplies. Thanks to her uncle's enlightened presidency, only a fraction of the cells were now inhabited. Even so, the stench of centuries of misery clung to the dim interior.

"This man you wish to speak to shares a cell with the other scum who use our people as mules to ferry their drugs," the captain told her. "I sent a guard to bring him to an interrogation room."

"Good."

She'd come up with some reason to get rid of both the captain and the guard. She wanted time alone with the prisoner to verify if he was, indeed, the man SPEAR had been seeking.

Flinging open a narrow door, her escort warned her to watch her head and stood to one side. Margarita ducked under the low lintel, took one step into the stark room and froze.

A red-faced guard stared at her through eyes bugged almost out of their sockets with terror. An arm was wrapped iron-tight around his throat. His gun holster flapped empty, and the barrel of his semiautomatic dug into his temple. Behind him, a horribly scarred figure smiled a malevolent welcome.

"Come in, Señorita de las Fuentes. I've been waiting for you."

Chapter 2

"Carlos?" Anna peered through the open doors of a small crimson and gold antechamber. "What are you doing in here all by yourself?"

"Looking for your cousin. Someone said they saw her come in here a while ago."

What looked suspiciously like a pout settled over Anna's delicate features for a moment. She chased it away with a toss of her dark hair. Slipping through the doors, she glided across the room.

"Won't I do instead?"

Instant alarms sounded in Carlos's head. Nubile and overripe for marriage, Anna had fixed her sights on him with almost the same determination he'd fixed his on Margarita. He suspected her determined pursuit sprang as much from jealousy of her cousin as from a young woman's infatuation with an older and decidedly more experienced male.

Another man might have been flattered by her attentions. A few might even have taken advantage of her passions. Carlos didn't feel the least temptation to accept the seductive invitations she insisted on sending his way. Anna was a pretty little thing, but she wasn't Margarita.

Smiling, he strolled across the plush carpet. "Let me escort you back to the ball. I have no doubt Miguel is looking for you to claim a dance."

"Miguel...pooh!" With a careless wave, she dismissed the lieutenant who served as Carlos's aide. "He's a boy. A mere boy."

"Actually, he's older than most lieutenants," Carlos countered mildly. "He worked his way up through the ranks and received his commission based solely on merit, not through family connections like so many."

"I don't wish to speak of Miguel." A sulky note crept into her voice. Slanting him a doe-eyed look through thick lashes, she slid her palms up his lapels. "I wish to speak of us."

Gently, he captured her wrists. "There is no us.

You know I've asked your uncle for Margarita's hand in marriage.''

"Yes, well, my cousin has a mind of her own when it comes to choosing her man. As do I.''

"So I've discovered," he said dryly. "Come, Miguel will be looking for you.''

"I don't want to dance with Miguel.'' Stubbornly, she dug in her heels. Her pout was real now. "If you must know, I saw Margarita leave the Palace almost an hour ago.''

"Did you?''

Well, well. That bit of information provided Carlos intense satisfaction. Evidently he wasn't the only one who'd needed some privacy to regroup from that shattering kiss they'd shared on the balcony.

"Did she say where she was going?''

"No.'' A sly expression slid across Anna's delicate features. "Perhaps she went to meet a lover.''

"I think not,'' he replied calmly.

In one of their more acerbic exchanges, Margarita had let Carlos know she wouldn't come to his bed a virgin...*if* the sky should fall and the mountains crumble and she one day decided to marry him. His jaw had locked at the idea of another man touching her, but he was honest enough to admit that he hadn't exactly spent the past thirty-eight years in a monastery.

He knew for a fact, however, that Rita's natural fastidiousness had kept her from forming any casual liaisons since her brief fling with another student during her years in the States. That gave him some consolation. As did the knowledge that her continued abstinence chafed her as much as it did him. She was a passionate woman, with the fire of her people in her veins...a fire Carlos was determined to stoke.

His body hardened once more at the mere thought of Margarita's mouth hot and eager under his. She wasn't as indifferent to him as she liked to pretend. She couldn't tremble at his touch, couldn't flush with heat the way she had, if she cared nothing for him.

Impatient to find her, Carlos tugged at Anna's clinging hands. He'd locate Margarita, escort her home, pick up where they'd left off on the balcony. And this time...

"Commandante!"

The urgent call whipped his head around. Although Carlos had given up both his uniform and the title he'd earned as commander of Madrileño's elite counterterrorism strike force when he accepted the post of deputy defense minister, old habits died hard. His military aide still called him commander, and Carlos still responded instinctively.

"Yes?"

Miguel Carreras hurried into the room. Short, sturdy and well muscled, the lieutenant admirably filled out his uniform adorned with a gold-roped aguillette and fancy dress sword.

"You must come at once, sir. There's been a…"

When he saw Anna clinging to Carlos's lapels, the lieutenant skidded to a stop. Surprise and hurt flickered in his brown eyes. Then his training kicked in and he turned a face of rocklike impassivity to his superior.

"There's been an incident at the *castillo.*"

"What kind of an incident?" Carlos asked, calmly disengaging Anna's hands. He hadn't missed that look of startled dismay on his aide's face. He'd talk to Miguel later and explain the situation, perhaps offer him some advice on handling Anna. Although he had to admit his own track record with the de las Fuentes women made him something less than an expert on the subject.

Stiffly ignoring the woman at his superior's side, Miguel poured out a hurried report. "I don't have all the details. Only that one of the prisoners was taken in for interrogation. He overwhelmed his guard and threatened to kill him. Margarita… Señorita de las Fuentes…offered herself as a hostage instead of the guard."

"What!"

Shock and disbelief slammed into Carlos. Every muscle in his body snapped wire taut.

"He took her with him," Miguel related with a worried frown. "Into the jungle. He commandeered a Jeep and took her with him."

The vicious curse that erupted from Carlos widened Anna's eyes.

"The captain of the guard just brought the word," the lieutenant finished. "He's waiting for you in the Gold Room."

Leaving an openmouthed Anna behind, Carlos strode through the doors. Questions hammered at him with each sharp crack of his heels on the parquet floors. What the devil was Margarita doing at the prison? Why had she offered herself as a hostage in the guard's place? Who was this prisoner who'd taken her?

While his mind whirled with unanswered questions, fear coiled in his gut. Margarita didn't know the jungle. She'd been raised in the city, spent her summers at her father's sugar plantation and years at school in the States. She'd never hacked her way through strangler vines as thick as a man's arm or dodged tarantulas the size of dinner plates. If by some stroke of luck she managed to escape this prisoner, she wouldn't last a day in the steaming green hell that covered most of Madrileño.

An icy sweat had pooled at the base of his spine

by the time Carlos strode into the Gold Room. At his entrance, the captain of the guard snapped to rigid attention, took one look at his murderous expression and blanched. Although democracy had taken firm root in Madrileño, most security matters—including the national police and administration of the prison system—came under the military, which was headed by the Minister of Defense. As deputy defense minister, Carlos stood in the captain's direct chain of command. He could have the man's head, or at least his pension, for this incident.

"You talk." He fired the words through clenched jaws. "I'll listen."

"We took this prisoner with the others in the big drug bust yesterday, the one we coordinated with the Americans."

"I'm aware of the operation," Carlos snapped.

He should be. After receiving a tip about a major heroine shipment being moved through the mountains to an isolated airstrip, he'd worked forty-eight hours straight to set up a multipronged, multinational attack. His men had taken down two planes, half-a-dozen aircrew members, a number of small-time drug lords and so many locals engaged in transporting the uncut heroin the police were still trying to sort them all out.

"This particular gringo would not tell us his

name," the captain reported. "He's an ugly bastard, very scarred, with one glass eye. We assumed
he was one of the fliers. When they asked us to
hold him in special custody—"

"*Who* asked you to hold him?"

The captain blinked at the whiplike question.
"The Americans, sir. We received a call...I assumed you knew."

Carlos would find out who made that call later.
Right now, his only concern was Margarita.

Unfortunately, the captain could shed no light
on why she'd asked to see this particular prisoner.
All he knew was that she'd showed up at the prison
and requested an interview.

"The gringo seemed to be expecting her. He
called her by name and smiled when she offered
herself as hostage instead of that sweating, sniv-
eling guard, as though he'd anticipated just such a
move."

Carlos stared at the captain, his face shuttered
while confusion piled on top of the fury gripping
at his chest. What the hell was going on here?
What had Margarita gotten involved in?

"The gringo left us locked in the interrogation
room," the captain confessed, shame evident in
every line of his stiff body. "The walls of the *castillo* are so thick, it was a good ten minutes before
anyone found us. My men report that Señorita de

las Fuentes walked out beside this man as though they were going for an evening stroll. Only after I was found did we discover that a Jeep was taken.''

"So no one saw which direction they headed?''

Miserable, the captain shook his head. "No, *commandante*.''

With some effort, Carlos held back another vicious curse. When he was satisfied that the captain could provide no further information, he dismissed him with a curt order to draw up a comprehensive plan to prevent such escapes in the future.

"Find Señor de las Fuentes,'' he snapped at Miguel. "Ask him to join me here.''

The lieutenant hurried away, leaving Carlos to think furiously. The certainty that there was more involved in yesterday's operation than a routine drug bust grew with each passing second. The tip had come at such an opportune moment. The support from the States had been too ready. And this call to the prison…

His face grim, he moved to an ornately carved console and snatched up the phone. He'd spent a few years in the States himself, first as a student at the Army's Command and General Staff College, then as a military attaché to the Madrileñan ambassador. He still had some friends in high circles. Some good friends.

By the time Margarita's anxious father hurried

into the reception room, Carlos was coldly, savagely furious. Even after four calls and several blunt reminders of Madrileño's unflagging support for America's antidrug campaign, he still didn't know who'd made the call. But he was determined to get to the bottom of it.

"What's going on?" her father demanded, puffing a bit from his quick walk.

A career bureaucrat, Eduard de las Fuentes had worked tirelessly to help his brother win the presidency and institute badly needed reforms. He was a good man, traditional in his family values but forward thinking when it came to his country's needs.

Succinctly, Carlos recounted the astounding events of the past half hour. Eduard gaped at him, his mouth popping open and closed like one of the orange-spotted frogs that populated the jungle.

"Margarita? This scum took my Margarita?"

"Apparently, she offered herself as hostage in exchange for the guard."

"But…but…why did she go to the prison in the first place?"

"I'll get the answer to that question when I find your daughter," Carlos promised grimly.

He'd get more than answers, he thought savagely as he strode down the Palace steps into the star-studded night. He'd bring her back safely and drag whatever information she had out of her. Then he'd either wring her neck for walking into this mess in the first place or tie her naked to his bed and keep her there until the blasted woman admitted she wanted him as much as he did her!

At the moment, the former option seemed infinitely more probable.

Within an hour he was back in uniform and had assembled his team.

Within two, he'd pulled together enough intelligence to indicate the escaped prisoner would in all likelihood head for a rendezvous point in the jungle, a cave hidden high in the mountains supposedly used as a way station by drug runners. There, he'd join forces with the heavily armed band that had reportedly been spotted crossing the border.

Worry for Margarita gnawing at his gut, Carlos sat beside his driver for the short ride to the military airbase just outside San Rico. Miguel and a small, handpicked squad of ten men followed in a half-ton truck. Although his aide had tried to hide his feelings behind a carefully blank mask, he hadn't yet recovered from the shock of finding Anna clinging like a limpet to his superior. Carlos would have to explain that scene to him—later!

When his mind was clear and fear for Margarita didn't crawl through his belly.

The helicopter crew had their bird preflighted and ready to go when Carlos and his team arrived at the airport. The squad filed to the chopper, almost invisible in their dark jungle fatigues and blackened faces. Silently, they climbed aboard and strapped in. While the rotor blades whirred and the engine whined up to full power, Carlos pulled a plastic-coated map from his pocket and ran through his hastily conceived tactical plan.

"We'll land here, a half mile to the west of the cave to avoid alerting anyone in the vicinity."

Stabbing a finger at the map, he pointed to an area devoid of towns, of plantations, of any signs of human habitation. The closest village lay a good ten miles to the west.

"With luck, we'll reach the cave ahead of the fugitive and his hostage and be waiting when they arrive. If by chance they get there before us, we'll use the element of surprise to come at them out of the darkness."

Either approach involved risk. To his men. To himself. To Margarita. Still, the plan was the best he could devise.

It might even have worked...if the helicopter hadn't developed engine trouble while they were still two miles from their objective. Using the chopper's powerful, million-candle-watt search-light, the cursing pilot found a hole in the jungle canopy at the last moment and put them down with only a bent rotor blade. Carlos jumped out and surveyed the solid wall of blackness beyond the searchlight's reach.

Two miles. They'd come down two miles from their planned landing zone, which put them two-and-a-half from the cave. On cleared terrain, he could run the distance in less than a half hour with full backpack. In the jungle, two and a half miles stretched to infinity.

Grimly, Carlos dug a pair of night-vision goggles from a pocket in his lightweight fatigue vest and led the way into dank, murky rain forest.

"Come on! Keep climbing!"

The gun barrel jabbed ruthlessly into Margarita's spine, prodding her up the steep path. She winced at the bruising pain, but it soon blended with all the others into an indistinguishable ache. Narrowing her eyes against the bright dawn haze, she inched her way up the path toward the distant roar of a waterfall.

With every stumbling step, needles of fire shot up her bound arms. Her shoulder sockets burned. Cramps pulled like iron tongs at calf muscles straining from the hard climb. At that moment, she

would have given almost everything she owned for
a few sips of water.

They'd driven all night, each twisting turn of the
road taking them higher into the mountains. For
the first hour or two of that long ride, Margarita
had listened with every sense straining for sounds
of pursuit. Hope of rescue faded with each grind
of the Jeep's gears. She should have known the
elusive criminal SPEAR had been hunting for
months would have planned his escape well.

Well, she wasn't going to make the escape any
easier for the walking piece of slime behind her.
Deliberately, she stumbled and went down on one
knee. Sharp rock cut into the jeans she'd hurriedly
thrown on before rushing to the prison. Her gasp
of pain was only half feigned.

"Get up!" her captor snarled, panting even
harder than Margarita from the arduous trek. He'd
emptied his canteen early in the climb. Thirst and
exertion put a rasp in his throat. "You're not fool-
ing anyone with this weak, helpless female act. I
know the kind of training you've had."

With an awkward twist of her upper body, Margarita propped a shoulder against the cliff face and
pushed herself up. Her breath cut like razor blades
into lungs starved for oxygen.

"How do you know what kind of training I've
had? Who are you?"

A sneer twisted his lips. "You tell me."

"All right." Her chest heaving, she propped her aching shoulders against the vine-covered rock wall behind her. "You're Simon."

"Very good." The sneer deepened, tugging at his scarred face. He stepped up beside her and dug the pistol barrel into the soft flesh under her chin. "And we both know who you are, don't we? The bitch who's been interfering in my operations in Central and South America."

With her back against sheer rock and a gun barrel grinding into the underside of her chin, Margarita weighed the odds of taking him down right then and there. If she twisted her head just a few inches to the right, hooked her shoulder into his chest and shoved the bastard over the side of the path before he got off a shot...

"It took me a while to figure out who Jonah had operating in Madrileño."

Jonah! The casual way he dropped the name froze Margarita in place. *Dios!* This man knew more about SPEAR than many of its own agents.

"What makes you think I work for Jonah?"

Vicious satisfaction laced his voice. "I have my ways of getting information...just as SPEAR does. You caused me considerable inconvenience, Señorita de las Fuentes. You and that bastard deputy defense minister."

"Carlos?"

Her surprised gasp drew a parody of a smile. "Yes, Carlos. Between the information you supplied SPEAR and Caballero's internal crackdown on the drug trade, the two of you just about destroyed my base of operations in this corner of the world."

Carlos! For the merest instant, she could hear his voice. Feel his mouth on hers. Just the thought of his strong, solid form brought the craven wish she'd never left his arms. Then reality returned in the form of a vicious killer.

"Good." Despite a throat parched with thirst, she managed a sarcastic smile. "I'm glad we inconvenienced you."

"I wouldn't look so pleased with yourself." The gun barrel ground into her jaw. "Your interference will end as of today."

Ignoring both the threat and the agony of steel against bone, she swept her captor a disdainful glance. His disfigurement had been startling enough in the dim prison interior. In the bright light of dawn, the puckered, angry flesh could weaken anyone's stomach. His glass eye remained fixed. His good eye followed hers as they roamed his scars.

"Hideous, aren't they?"

She refused to give him so much as a hint of sympathy. "I've seen worse."

With the cosmetic techniques available today, he could have had the scars removed. That he chose not to told her he took some kind of perverse pride in his disfigurement—or that he wanted a bitter daily reminder of whatever cataclysmic event had caused it. When she suggested as much in a cool voice, something so evil flared in his one good eye that Margarita's palms flattened against rock behind her.

"I want Jonah to see them. Which he will...and soon. Now move it, Señorita. I've wasted enough time in this stinking green cesspool you call a country."

The slur to Madrileño only added to his hostage's growing determination to shove his gun barrel between his teeth and make him eat his words along with a good six inches of cold steel. Laughing at the deadly promise in her eyes, he stepped back and motioned her onward. With her chin bruised and fire burning in her heart, Margarita resumed her climb.

Her chance would come.

It had to come.

The path twisted and turned. The sun crawled higher, a blazing ball visible through gaps in the vines and trees clinging to the mountain. Twice, Margarita stumbled to her knees, only to be jerked upright by a cruel hand in her hair. Once, the little locket stuck to the sweaty skin beneath her blouse began to vibrate.

The feel of it humming against her breasts made her want to weep with frustration. The tiny device hidden inside only received signals, didn't send them. There was no way for SPEAR to pinpoint her location.

Gradually, the roar of the waterfall grew louder. When they rounded a bend and Simon dragged back a straggling curtain of vines to reveal a gaping hole in the cliff face, Margarita knew time was running out. She'd have to free herself quickly, before his accomplices appeared on the scene and her value as a hostage ended.

With a grunt, he planted a fist in her back and shoved her inside the cave. She made a frantic sweep of the dank interior for snakes or other inhospitable inhabitants before she hit the rock floor. The thud jarred her teeth. Cursing fluently in both Spanish and English, she twisted up and around.

"My friends will be here shortly," he said with callous indifference to her curses. "While we wait, I'll fill the canteen at the waterfall."

Swiping his forearm across his sweaty forehead, he dragged another length of rope from his back pocket and tied her ankles. He seemed to take particular delight in yanking the knots until they cut almost through her boot tops. Margarita refused to so much as move a muscle at his rough treatment, even when he slid his palm up her calf and squeezed, hard.

"Be a good girl and I'll give you some water."

A smile dragged at his misshapen mouth. His hand roamed higher, to her thigh. She felt its damp heat through her jeans.

"Then again, maybe I won't. Maybe you'll have to beg for it. I like my women hot and desperate."

"I imagine that's the only way a scum like you can get them."

His casual backhand snapped her head back. She tasted blood…and the absolute conviction that she'd see this man in hell before he touched her again.

"You'll beg," he predicted with a sneering confidence that ground her teeth together. "Long and hard."

The son of a pig!

The moment he disappeared through the vines, Margarita dragged herself up and began searching the cave. All she needed was a ragged edge, a sharp protuberance of any kind to saw through her bonds. She'd wiggled her way out of worse situations than this during SPEAR's brutal escape and evasion training.

That was training, a nasty little voice inside her head heckled. *This is for real.*

As if she needed the reminder! Ignoring the scream of protest from her shoulders, Margarita rolled over to the nearest wall and fumbled behind her with numbed fingers for its surface. Panic rose in waves when she felt nothing but smooth rock. Choking with frustration, she humped and stretched and humped again, propelling herself snail-like along the floor, searching the surface behind her with desperate fingers.

She'd almost given up hope when she scraped against a small, sharp crack in the rock. Praying its flintlike edge would do the job, she pushed up on one elbow to gain leverage and went to work. Her back arched at an awkward angle. Every back-and-forth movement caused a white-hot lance of pain in her shoulders. Sweat ran in rivulets from her temples. Blood dripped onto her balled fists from wrists scraped raw by rope and stone.

Straining, grunting, sawing, Margarita struggled to keep track of the passing seconds. Her heart hammered as she listened for the thud of footsteps, but she knew she'd never hear Simon's return over the thundering falls and her jackhammering pulse.

When the ropes finally parted, what began as a

fervent prayer of thanksgiving spiraled instantly into a silent scream. For several precious moments, Margarita could only writhe on the cave floor while her abused shoulder sockets exacted their revenge. Finally, the agony subsided enough for her to sit up. Panting, she fumbled at the ropes binding her ankles. When they, too, gave, she dropped her forehead onto her knees and allowed herself one moment of sobbing relief.

Not a heartbeat later, the faint scrape of rock on rock brought her head up with a jerk. Molten fury coursed through Margarita. This time, she wouldn't hand herself over so easily. This time, she'd have a few surprises in store for a certain one-eyed bastard.

She was gathering herself for an attack when gunfire burst out in the valley below. Her heart contracted painfully as monkeys screamed and birds flapped noisily into the sky. In almost the same instant, a shadowy figure appeared at the curtain of vines draped across the cave's mouth.

She caught the glitter of sunlight on a gun barrel. With a feral snarl, Margarita launched herself through the vines.

Chapter 3

Long afterward, Carlos would shudder every time he remembered the violence that suddenly erupted at the cave's mouth.

One moment, he was feeling his way cautiously along the narrow path, searching for the entrance to the cave. The next, a burst of gunfire told him the squad he'd positioned to guard the approach to the steep track had engaged with a hostile force.

Then a dark fury exploded through vines straggling down the cliff face and catapulted into Carlos. Only the fact that he'd inched his way up the dangerous track with every sense on full alert kept him from being butted right off the path and over the sheer cliff.

In a purely self-protective move, Carlos grappled with his attacker and flung them both sideways, away from the edge of the precipice. Struggling furiously, they went down in a tangle of thrashing arms and legs. A vicious elbow dug into his windpipe. Choking, Carlos wrenched an arm free and pulled it back. His balled fist was in midswing when his attacker flung back a tangled mass of ebony hair and snarled a curse.

"Son of a motherless—!"

Violet eyes widened in shock. Just in time, Carlos pulled his punch. The blow slammed into her shoulder instead her jaw. With a small, helpless cry of agony, she crumpled onto his chest.

"Dios!"

Rolling them both away from the edge of the track, Carlos scrambled to his knees. His first instinct was to gather her writhing form into his arms and pour out a thousand apologies for the brutal blow, but the soldier in him needed to secure the area first.

Shaking his head to clear it, he performed a swift mental assessment of the situation. The stutter of guns behind and below them told him his men were engaged in a full-fledged firefight. He had no idea how many enemy were coming up the path and how many might already be in the cave. Given his vulnerable position on the narrow ledge, attack was his only defense.

With a warning to Margarita to stay low, he took a firm grip on his 9 mm Beretta, threw himself through the vines, and hit the floor rolling. An instant later, he was on his feet, sweeping the cave with savage eyes. Only after he was satisfied it held no immediate threat did he jam his pistol into its holster and rush outside. His throat closed when he saw the way Margarita had curled into a fetal ball against the cliff face.

"Rita! Sweetheart!" Gently, he rolled her over. "I'm so sorry! I didn't know it was you."

"Ob...viously."

Biting down on her lower lip, she struggled to sit up. Tears streaked her dirt-smudged cheeks. Leaves and bits of debris clung to her tumbled hair and long-sleeved white shirt. When Carlos spotted the bright red blood staining her sleeves, his heart stopped.

"What did that bastard do to—"

Crack!

Rock splintered a mere six inches from his face. The shot was still reverberating when Carlos threw himself forward, shielding Margarita's body with his own. A burst of fire followed the first bullet, each one sending vicious rock shards flying through the air.

It took less than a heartbeat for him to realize these shots came not from the path below, but from the direction of the waterfall he heard rumbling in the distance beyond the cave. In a lightning reflex, he banded an arm around Margarita's waist and half dragged, half flung her around a bend in the path. A stone outcropping protected them from the shooter momentarily.

"It's him!" she gasped. "The escaped prisoner! He's got the submachine gun he took from the guard."

On his own, Carlos wouldn't have thought twice about tackling the man. But he wasn't on his own, and the driving necessity right now was to remove Margarita from the line of fire.

His men were strung out along the path below, fighting a ferocious rearguard action from the sound of it. The dangerous fugitive was above and closing fast. They couldn't stay in this exposed position. That left only one option.

"We're going over the side."

She shot a wide-eyed glance at the steep precipice, gulped and nodded. Whipping off his belt, Carlos slapped it around her waist and slid the tongue through the buckle. A quick tug yanked it tight.

"Grab the vines to break your slide," he ordered, wrapping the loose end of the webbing around his fist. "I'll do the same."

Another burst of fire plowed into the rock less than a foot away. Carlos ducked, muttered an oath that was half curse, half prayer and dragged her with him over the edge.

Their plunging descent could only have lasted seconds, but to Margarita it seemed like a lifetime. Spongy vegetation shielded their bodies from the worst of the cliff face, and Carlos's raw strength kept them from a disastrous free fall. Somehow, he managed to lock his fist around vines that stretched like elastic bands with their weight. Just as one vine reached the breaking point, he made a frantic grab for another.

Margarita heard him grunt with the strain of hanging onto both her tether and his precarious handholds while the two of them bumped and slithered down the slope. To her disgust, she could do little to help. Her right arm dangled uselessly, still numb from the combined effects of his savage blow and hours twisted behind her back. Her left arm had tangled in the belt anchoring her to Carlos.

At last the slope gentled enough for him to drag them both to a halt. They lay on their backs for a few seconds, panting. She couldn't get her breath, could barely see for the sweat stinging her eyes. Twisting, she swiped her face on her sleeve and stared upward.

A multitude of green layers shielded them from observation. The thunder of the falls was the only sound that penetrated the dense stillness. His chest heaving, Carlos rolled to his feet and tugged Margarita up.

"Are you all right?"

"I will be." She clawed at the belt cutting her in two. "Once I…can breathe…again."

"Here, let me."

His big hands fumbled with the buckle. When the tortuous constriction around her middle loosened, she gulped in long swallows of air.

His face grim, Carlos hitched the belt around his hips and swiped an arm across his face. For the first time, Margarita noticed he'd donned the mottled green and black of jungle fatigues. Over a similarly camouflaged long-sleeved shirt and black T-shirt, he wore a nylon vest with dozens of little pockets. Streaks of black and green face paint smudged to a muddy mask made him almost indistinguishable from the jungle around him.

No wonder she hadn't recognized him when she dived headfirst through the vines! She'd seen him in his dress uniform dozens of times before he resigned his military commission to accept the dep-

uty minister's job, and in impeccable civilian attire
ever since. But this was the first time she'd
glimpsed the soldier in his element. He looked almost like a stranger.

Even his voice sounded different. Cold and flat,
it lacked any hint of inflection. All traces of the
teasing note he generally employed with her had
completely disappeared. Belatedly, Margarita realized he was holding himself in rigid check.

How in God's name did he do it? Every emotion
from wild elation at having escaped to bitter self-
disgust for not taking Simon down tumbled
through her. Carlos apparently could mount a
search-and-rescue effort, dodge a hail of bullets,
plunge down a mountainside and still exercise a
self-discipline that amazed and, perversely, irritated her no end.

"Stay here," he ordered, reaching once more for
a long, straggling vine. "I'm going back up to regroup my men. I'll drop a rope down for you when
we have the situation under control."

Margarita's eyes narrowed. If he thought she
was going to sit here meekly and wait with hands
folded, he'd better think again. She'd just opened
her mouth to set him straight when a little splat
sounded a few feet away. It was followed in the
next instant by the distant crack of a rifle. Another

series of splats set a feathery fern trembling just above her head.

"God!"

Releasing the vine, Carlos lunged for her. No dummy, Margarita was already diving for the shelter of a rotting log.

"There!" The echo of a shout came through the canopy. "I see a flash of white."

Within the blink of an eye, a deadly hail of bullets tore through the dense canopy of leaves. The crumbling log provided no protection at all. Hauling Margarita upright by her wrist, Carlos took off. His grip was brutal on flesh already raw and bleeding from being scraped against sharp rock, but she was in no mind to protest as they broke into a desperate run.

Bullets ripped through leaves just above their heads. Twice more, they heard shouts. Once, a scream and what sounded like the thrashing fall of a body down the mountainside behind them. Then the jungle swallowed all sounds. Ferns the size of small trees whipped at Margarita's face and arms. Dangling vines tried to trip her. Spiky pineapple plants and tank bromeliads tore at her blouse.

By the time they reached the lower slopes, a painful stitch stabbed into her side, her wrist was bleeding again, and every breath singed her lungs. Thankfully, the underbrush thinned out enough to make the going at this level a little easier. Instead of lush plants, the jungle floor consisted primarily of fallen tree trunks, leafy ferns and layers of rotting vegetation.

Margarita knew this lack of undergrowth was due to the giant strangler figs, which began life as seeds dropped by monkeys or birds in the branches of host trees. The stranglers then sprouted roots that dropped ropelike to the ground, forming a sort of cage around their host. Their trunks shot upward and spread dense green umbrellas of leaves. In the process, these monstrous kings of the rain forest starved their host trees of light. Eventually, all that was left beneath the canopy were the rotting remains of host trees covered with luminous green mosses, ferns and flashy flowers like the orchids that clung in great clumps to the tree trunks.

Margarita had no idea how far they traveled through this dim, green gloom before Carlos at last signaled a halt. He stood silent, head up, eyes narrowed, listening intently for sounds of pursuit. At that moment, Margarita couldn't have heard an elephant crashing through the forest over her own wheezing breath. Bending at the waist, she planted her sweaty palms on thighs that quivered like overstretched elastic and dragged air into her aching lungs.

"I think we've lost them."

The hoarse timbre of his voice drew her upright. Slanting Carlos a quick glance, she saw that sweat had plastered his black hair to his head. His chest heaved under his fatigue shirt. He, too, sucked in long gulps of air. Unaccountably pleased that he was feeling the effects of that break-neck run as much as she was, Margarita summoned a shaky smile.

"The bullets started flying back there before I could thank you for coming after me."

"Thank me?" His head snapped around. "*Thank* me!"

Her grin slipped, then disappeared completely as he rounded on her. As dangerous as a panther prodded from its den and twice as furious, he stalked across the spongy carpet of vegetation.

"I don't want your thanks."

The sparks shooting from his black eyes set Margarita's back up. She'd been through too much in the past twelve hours to take that tone from him or anyone else.

"Fine! You don't want my thanks. Then I suggest you use that radio attached to your belt to call your men and arrange a rendezvous." She turned away, intending to find some water for her parched throat. "In the meantime, I'll…"

He planted himself in front of her, blocking the way. "There are only two things I want from you at this moment. The first is an explanation. What the hell's going on?'' he demanded, his dark gaze drilling into her. ''Why did you go to the prison last night?''

Unfortunately, she couldn't give him an explanation even if she wanted to. Like all SPEAR agents, Margarita had sworn an oath of secrecy about her membership in the elite cadre. From the thunderous expression on Carlos's face, she guessed she'd have to do some fast talking to get him to buy the cover story she'd fabricated for the captain of the guard at the *castillo*.

''It's my job to analyze the impact of the illegal drug trade on our nation's economy, remember? This fugitive is obviously a key figure in that trade. I thought he might let something slip that would give me a clearer picture of what we're dealing with.''

She could see Carlos wasn't buying it. Disbelief showed clearly under the streaks of black face paint still decorating his cheeks and chin.

''Do you expect me to believe you left a dress ball to speak with a prisoner you could have interviewed just as easily the next morning?''

She tipped her chin and looked him square in the eye. ''There was nothing to keep me at the ball. I was bored and decided to leave.''

The barb hit home. His jaw clenched. A vein

throbbed amid the taut cords of his neck. He stared at her with such glittering intensity that Margarita felt a flutter of something close to nervousness.

This was Carlos, she reminded herself. Always in control Carlos. Much as he probably wanted to throttle her at this particular moment, he'd rein in the emotions simmering behind his scowl.

To her secret disappointment, he did.

"The captain of the guard said this prisoner recognized you the moment you walked in the door," he ground out. "How did he know your name?"

"The same way he knew yours, I'd guess," she shot back.

"Mine?"

"In one of his more pleasant moments, he admitted that your raids had just about destroyed his base of operations in Madrileño."

That, at least, afforded Carlos some measure of satisfaction. If she thought she'd bought her way out of further questions with the welcome information, however, she soon learned otherwise. His razor-edged gaze raked her sweaty face.

"What game are you playing, Margarita?"

"None."

She justified her stiff reply with the silent argument that no one in their right mind would classify the events of the past twelve hours as a game.

Carlos stepped closer, and Margarita battled the

ridiculous urge to back away. She'd never dreamed
he could project such intimidating authority with a
single, narrow-eyed look.

Evidently what he saw in her face satisfied him
for the moment. Or so she concluded from his
scathing comment about pigheaded females who
take their job with the Ministry of Economics too
damned seriously for their own or anyone else's
good.

Stung, Margarita lifted her chin. "Perhaps I take
my job seriously because I prefer to do something
useful with my life instead of just sit at home like
a good little Madrileñan wife."

"Something useful?" he shot back sarcastically.
"Like offering yourself as a hostage? What in
God's name persuaded you into that bit of lu-
nacy?"

"I couldn't let him kill the guard in cold
blood."

"So instead you let him take you! My heart
stopped when I heard you'd gone with him."

She was still digesting that interesting bit of information when icy fury surged into his face. Apparently her seemingly reckless action angered
Carlos as much or more as he claimed it had worried him last night.

"You little fool, what would you have done if
I hadn't come after you?"

"Just what I did do," she retorted. "Escape. Are you forgetting that I was on my way *out* of the cave when you were on your way *in?*"

"No, and I'm not forgetting how you crumpled like a deflated balloon when I struck your shoulder! You wouldn't have stood a chance if this prisoner had taken it into his head to rape you as well as use you as a hostage."

She decided this wasn't the time to tell him Simon had entertained exactly that thought. Or that Carlos's blow to her shoulder had caught her at a decidedly weak moment.

"We'll talk about how you managed to escape later," he said tightly. "Right now…"

"Yes?"

He didn't answer for a moment. Margarita sensed he was waging a fierce inner battle to contain the anger that still glittered in his eyes. Some deep-seated feminine instinct warned her not to goad him further. An even deeper instinct prodded her into recklessness.

"You said you wanted two things from me," she reminded him impatiently. "What's the second?"

The bite in her voice snapped his brows together. Margarita caught a flash of something dangerous in his eyes. She had time for only a half step back before he wrapped an arm around her waist and hauled her against him.

"This."

His mouth ground down on hers with a savagery that stunned her. The force of the kiss bent her backward. The fist Carlos tangled in her hair dragged her head back even further.

She knew a moment of heady exultation. This wasn't the same man who'd courted her with such deliberate, sensual intent on a moonlit balcony just last night. Smooth, sophisticated, rigidly controlled, that man had always held a part of himself back.

This one held *nothing* back.

This kiss was wild. Raw. Primitive. A searing fusion of mouths and chests and straining thighs.

A part of her acknowledged that adrenaline no doubt still pumped through him as fiercely as it did her. That the closeness of their escape had wound his nerves as tight as a steel spring. He needed release. So did she.

It took a moment for Margarita to realize he wasn't seeking her participation in this intense ritual. Like a medieval knight, he'd stormed the enemy's stronghold, carried off his prize and now claimed her.

Somehow, this wasn't quite the reaction she'd anticipated when she envisioned shattering his formidable self-discipline at last. She didn't want to be claimed any more than she wanted to be protected. With Carlos's mouth hot and hard on hers, however, she was beginning to wonder just what in heaven's name she *did* want!

She was as confused as she was angry when he finally released her. Cheeks hot, eyes cold, she looked him up and down.

"Much as I'd like to, I'm not going to flatten you for that little display of masculine aggression."

The sardonic lift of one dark brow invited her to try. Only the fact that Margarita owed him for coming after her kept her from doing just that.

"We'll continue this discussion when we get back to San Rico," he stated, pulling a small radio out of one of the pockets on his camouflage-patterned vest.

"Will we?"

"Yes."

The absolute implacability in the single word raised Margarita's hackles all over again. This wasn't the time or the place to argue with him, however. Not with the memory of that rain of bullets ripping through the leaves still so vivid. The first order of business was to get them out of here.

Which, they discovered when Carlos extracted his radio, might present some difficulties. Frowning, he adjusted the telescoping antenna and tried again. The digital display remained blank. His mouth twisting in disgust, he snapped the antenna down.

"The damned thing is supposed to withstand combat drops from high-altitude aircraft. It couldn't even take a tumble down a mountainside."

Frustration ate at Margarita. He couldn't communicate with his men, and she couldn't communicate with SPEAR. Worried about the damned metal detectors, she'd left her purse containing her radio and little Smith and Wesson snub-nosed revolver at the prison entrance checkpoint last night. As far as she knew, they were still there. The only piece of equipment she carried was the locket on the gold chain that had, somehow, survived the wild slide down the mountain.

Carlos echoed her frustration as he shoved his radio into its case. "Looks like we walk."

"Back along the road?"

He considered and dismissed the easy route in one shake of his head. "Without knowing who won the firefight we just heard, we can't risk it. We'll have to strike out in the opposite direction and try for the nearest village."

"How near is near?"

''Ten miles.''

Gulping, Margarita swept the dank, silent rain forest with a searching glance. If there was a track through the green maze, she couldn't see it.

Chapter 4

Faced with the threat of Simon behind and a daunting trek ahead, Margarita's training kicked in.

"We'd better take an inventory of what we've got with us before we start walking. Just in case," she added with a shrug when Carlos shot her a swift look. "Anything can happen in the jungle."

She might not be able to tell him about Simon or her SPEAR background, but she was darned if she'd act the helpless, bubbleheaded female.

Nodding, he slipped out of his lightweight vest and hunkered down on one heel. Margarita joined him, listening intently as he opened the various pouches and detailed their contents.

"I designed this modified jungle kit when I commanded the counterterrorist strike force. It's geared for swift travel through this type of terrain and attack rather than extended operations."

Margarita grasped at once the incisive thinking that had gone into the kit. In addition to a machete tucked into a built-in scabbard, the pack contained the essentials for short-term survival in the jungle. Included were a mosquito net folded into a square the size of a cigarette pack; a large-mouthed plastic bag to capture fresh rainwater and thus avoid the dangers of larvae-infested groundwater; a Global Positioning Satellite directional finder; night-vision goggles that folded flat; a Swiss army knife with its myriad utensils; a first aid kit; spare ammunition clips; and an extra pair of socks. As mundane as the last item might seem to the outsider, Margarita knew well that foot rot had crippled many a soldier slogging through her country's tropical rain forests.

She paid scant attention to the machete. The razor-edged blade constituted a familiar household item in Madrileño. But the black steel automatic he slid out of its holster and laid across his palm snagged her instant and undivided attention.

"This is a standard Army-issue Beretta. I've had the barrel shortened to my specifications."

Margarita didn't volunteer the fact that she'd qualified at the expert level with a weapon very similar to this one. A Model 92D double action, to be exact, with a slick slide, no external safety and a bobbed hammer.

"The clip holds ten rounds." In a move of practiced economy, Carlos slid out the magazine, checked its spring-loaded contents and snapped it into place. "With one round in the chamber, that gives you—"

"Eleven. I can add. I can also shoot. My father taught me one summer," she said in answer to his questioning look. "We'd hold target practice in the canebrakes at the sugar plantation."

She didn't see any need to add that she was only eight at the time and barely big enough to shoulder her father's double-barrel shotgun. Or that he'd only indulged her a single time, on a whim. Her mother had taken one look at Margarita's bruised collarbone and ended such nonsense then and there.

Grimly, Carlos holstered the weapon. "Let's hope you won't have to put your target practice to use."

She didn't answer, her mind on the brief inventory just conducted. Her would-be suitor had set out last night well equipped for any eventuality...unlike a certain SPEAR agent, she thought wryly. Once again she cursed the metal detectors at the prison.

At least she'd had the sense to change out of her gown into boots and jeans before her quick dash to the *castillo* last night, although she wished she'd chosen something sturdier than this long-sleeved white cotton blouse. Her close encounters with the rocky mountain slope had almost shredded the darned thing. Thoroughly disgusted with herself for landing in this situation so unprepared, Margarita pushed to her feet.

Her first priority was to get back to civilization and contact SPEAR. With luck, they could still mount a containment search that would net the elusive Simon. She also wanted to relay to Jonah the few bits of information she'd managed to extract. Simon knew who headed SPEAR, he wore his scars like a badge and he planned for Jonah to see them...soon.

"We'd better get moving," she said, raking back her tangled hair.

"In a minute. I want to take a look at your wrists first."

"They've stopped bleeding." Impatiently, she tore a strip off her tattered shirttail. "I'll cover the abrasions with this to protect them from mosquitoes and—"

"Let me look at them."

Just in time, Margarita caught back a sharp protest. Common sense dictated that she let him doctor

the wounds. Even an untended scratch could lead
to disaster in the jungle. Yet she wasn't quite ready
for Carlos to touch her again. She still hadn't
sorted the confusion he'd generated a few moments
ago with that shattering kiss. Just the prospect of
his hands on her made her distinctly uncomfortable. As a result, she conceded with something less
than graciousness.

He lifted her left arm and rolled back her sleeve
to inspect the damage. At the sight of the raw,
oozing flesh, Carlos sucked in a swift breath and
Margarita gulped. The ugly wounds looked even
worse than they felt, which took some doing!

"I've got some antiseptic powder in the first aid
kit," he told her, frowning. "It'll help prevent in-
fection. Take off your shirt."

"Excuse me?"

"We'll need it for bandages." When still she
hesitated, his voice took on a sardonic note. "In
case you haven't noticed, it's not good for much
else."

She'd noticed, but the actual extent of her near-
nakedness didn't sink in until Carlos dropped his
gaze from her face to the swell of her breasts,
clearly visible through the torn cotton. Heat
crawled into Margarita's cheeks when she glanced
down and saw what had engaged his unabashed
interest.

In her rush to the prison, she'd traded her gown for jeans but hadn't bothered to change her undies. She still wore the red lace bikini panties and wisp of a bra fitted with convenient little push-up pads that transformed her modest curves into seductive mounds.

She'd forked over a small fortune for the scraps of lace. From the glint in Carlos's eyes, the money was well spent. Flashing her a wicked grin, he reached into his pocket for the first aid kit.

"I think I told you last night that I like you in red."

"Did you?" Margarita tossed off a shrug. "I don't recall."

The dart failed to penetrate his impervious hide. Still grinning, he ripped a corner off the packet with strong, white teeth.

"Take off your shirt."

Without another word, she yanked open the few buttons still left on the blouse and shrugged out of the mangled garment. Feeling ridiculously exposed in only her bra and the little locket, she extended her wrist. He held it gently while he tapped a generous amount of powder onto the oozing wounds.

"Dios!" Hissing, Margarita fought the urge to snatch her hand free and smack him. "You might have warned me the treatment is even worse than the injury!"

"You would've just tensed up in anticipation. Now you know the worst. Hold still."

With that calm, callous order, he bent his head and sprinkled the powder along the circlet of rope burns. Margarita saw bits of green nested in his glossy hair. As they no doubt did in hers. A frown of concentration creased his brow. Thick black lashes screened his eyes.

Once more she was struck by the difference between this man and the Carlos she knew. The smooth, sophisticated politician who'd wooed her with such deliberation had disappeared. In his place was a lean, bronzed jungle warrior...one who displayed a lamentable tendency to issue orders.

"Give me your other hand."

Catching her lower lip hard between her teeth, Margarita complied. This time she was prepared for the flash of fire that seared her flesh. Almost.

She was gritting her teeth when he ripped what was left of her shirt into long strips and wrapped them loosely around her wrists. Tucking in the ends, he surveyed his handiwork with a critical eye.

"That should do it."

His gaze traveled from her wrist to her face, with an intermittent stop in the vicinity of her breasts.

An unnecessarily protracted intermittent stop, Margarita thought indignantly.

"You always wear that locket," he observed, as though he was admiring the modest piece of jewelry instead of the mounded flesh it nestled between. "Does it hold some special sentimental value for you?"

"Very special," she replied coolly, refusing to react to the gleam in his eyes as they lingered on her pushed-up curves. With obvious reluctance, he brought his gaze to meet hers.

"You can't travel like that. The mosquitoes will eat you alive." Unbuttoning his long-sleeved jungle fatigue blouse, he shrugged out of it. Muscles rippled under his black T-shirt as he held the outer garment for her to slip into.

"You'll need protection, too," she protested. Although the mosquitoes that plagued her country swarmed mostly at dawn and early evening, they could make life miserable for anyone who worked outside.

"I'll smear some mud on my forearms. I've found that works as well as any repellent. Come, Rita, we're wasting time."

Still Margarita hesitated. Some primitive sixth sense screamed at her not to envelop herself in his warmth and his scent. The image flashed into her mind once more of a sleek, black panther, his coiled muscles rippling as he rubbed against his mate to mark her with his spoor and warn off all other interested males. Try as she might, she couldn't shake the absurd notion that stripping off her own shirt had constituted the first step in some sort of primal mating ritual. Sliding her arms into Carlos's would constitute the second.

His intent, hooded gaze as he waited for her to take that small step didn't exactly soothe her frazzled nerves. With a vague sense of unease, Margarita recognized that the delicate balance of power between them had somehow shifted dramatically. Mere hours ago, she'd strolled off and left him cooling his heels on a deserted balcony.

Now...

Now, she thought on a spurt of impatience, this dim, primeval jungle was doing a serious number on her imagination and her common sense. She could hardly traipse for miles with only a scrap of red lace to protect her from dive-bombing mosquitoes.

"Thanks," she muttered, thrusting her arms into the lightweight shirt decorated in mottled green and black. He settled the garment across her shoulders.

"You're welcome."

His warm breath ruffled the hair at her temple

and tickled her ear. Instant shivers raced down Margarita's spine.

For pity's sake! She needed to get a grip here. Shoving the buttons through the holes on the fatigue shirt, she forced her mind to focus on the very real matter of their survival.

"Do you have any idea how to get to this village you mentioned?"

Nodding, Carlos extracted a small, flat case from his vest pocket. "I memorized the coordinates. This little baby will get us where we need to go…if it held up better than the damned radio," he added under his breath.

They both breathed sighs of relief when the handheld receiver came to life with a quiet beep. Although she didn't say so, Margarita recognized the device immediately. The tiny receiver contained a specialized computer that received signals from NAVSTAR satellites, keystones of the Global Positioning System originally developed by the United States Department of Defense. Military and civilian navigational systems throughout the world used GPS to calculate locations to within a few meters.

The receiver beeped again. Frowning, Carlos did a rapid mental calculation.

"We're exactly ten and a quarter miles north-northwest from the village."

The unpalatable fact that they were so far from civilization didn't improve with repetition.

"Ten and a quarter miles as the crow flies," he corrected. "*If* a crow or any other bird could fly a straight line through the jungle. Are you ready?"

She swept the jungle ahead with another look, drew in a deep breath and nodded.

Sliding his machete free of its scabbard, Carlos took the lead. For all of a moment or two, Margarita thought about challenging his automatic assumption of command. As quickly as the thought occurred, she dismissed it. The trek through the jungle wasn't a matter of sexual politics. It was a matter of survival. She'd contribute to their journey in whatever way she could.

The going was even tougher than she expected.

The dense canopy shut out most of the sunlight. Ropelike vines draped from the towering trees, so thick in places that Carlos had to hack through them. Beneath the high canopy, the forest floor was covered with rotting vegetation topped by layers of mossy mold five or six inches thick. The greenish slime sucked at Margarita's boots with every step and soon had her calf muscles screaming in protest.

Steep slopes and plunging ravines made traveling on a straight line impossible. They headed south, then east, then doubled back to the west so many times Margarita soon lost any sense of direction. The rainstorms that burst without warning overhead and needled through the canopy didn't help matters, either. Her clothes were still steaming from a late morning shower when an early afternoon storm drenched her all over again.

Despite the discomforts of the walk, she couldn't help but drink in the raw, secret beauty around her. Clouds of red and gold butterflies dazzled her. Brilliant turquoise and purple parrots swooped through the trees. Orchids the size of bridal bouquets dangled from vines and tree trunks, contributing both color and fragrance to the scene.

As the day wore on, she came to appreciate the statistics she'd absorbed intellectually over the years about the jungle they traversed. It covered almost four-fifths of Madrileño, varying from the rain-soaked cloud forests atop the highest peaks to the lush tropical vegetation of the lower slopes. More than a hundred rivers and streams tumbled down the mountains and crisscrossed the jungle before emptying into the sea. Just last year, a professor at the University of San Rico had catalogued seven different species of insects that existed nowhere else on earth but Madrileño.

Reading about these insects and encountering them face-to-face were two different matters, however. She managed not to shriek—barely!—when she ducked behind a tree to relieve herself and the largest spider she'd ever seen crawled out from under some leaf litter to observe the process. The thing looked like a Frisbee, with a body at least six inches in diameter and a leg span of more than twelve inches. Margarita beat a hasty and exceptionally undignified retreat, leaving the field to the black monster.

Her skin still crawled with distaste when a different sensation suddenly made her nerve endings jump. She stopped in her tracks and slapped a hand to her chest. The sharp sound spun Carlos around.

"What is it?"

"Nothing," she lied as the locket vibrated under her sweaty palm. "A mosquito."

Nodding, he turned to lead the way again. Frustration ate at Margarita as she trudged after him. If only she could contact SPEAR. Jonah must have received a full account of the night's activities by now. He'd be as anxious to know she'd survived the kidnapping and firefight as she was to report in. Worry over how she'd get word to SPEAR shoved all thoughts of the spider out of her head.

Unfortunately, the black monster wasn't the only unpleasant creature Margarita encountered that afternoon. During the break Carlos insisted on later in the day, she almost sat on another. She knew enough to kick the fallen tree trunk she chose as a seat to dislodge any resident scorpions. But she wasn't prepared for Carlos's laconic warning when she sank down with a weary sigh.

"Watch out. That *Mycetozoa* will crawl right up your leg."

She sprang up, searching frantically for some hairy insect with oversize mandibles and a nasty gleam in its eye. All she spotted was a slippery dark mass on the underside of the log.

"All right," she snapped at a grinning Carlos. "Where and what is this my-see-a-thing?"

"Mycetozoa." Still grinning, he strolled over and hunkered down beside the log. "That's the scientific name for it. Most people just call it slime mold. It's a curious little creature, half fungus and half animal."

Gathering a gooey green blob onto a fingertip, he held it up for her inspection.

"The fungus feeds on bacteria in the rotting wood as it oozes upward to catch some light. Once in the light, it sprouts into these flowerlike filaments and release spores. Here, take a look."

The slimy blob didn't hold the same fascination for Margarita it evidently held for Carlos. Firmly, she declined his invitation.

"I can see it from here, thanks."

"Wind, rain or passing animals will spread the

spores, which each contain a living cell. The cells then attach to a damp surface, split like an amoeba and start forming a brand-new slime mold.''

"Just what the world needs,'' she drawled. "More slime mold.''

Laughing, Carlos swiped the green gob off his finger and rose. "It has its uses, *querida.*''

"If one of those uses isn't providing sustenance for humans, I'm not interested.''

He quirked a brow. "Are you trying to say you're hungry?''

"A little,'' she replied with magnificent under-statement. The bacon-wrapped shrimp canapés she'd nibbled on at the reception before last night's ball had long since passed through her digestive tract. She'd snatched enough sips of water from the streams they'd passed to quell the worst of her hunger pangs, but tantalizing images of hearty bowls of black beans or the sizzling beef strips street vendors grilled on every corner in San Rico were starting to dance in her mind.

"Can you hold out a little longer?'' Carlos asked with a small frown. "I'd like to keep trav-eling as long as we have light.''

Resolutely, she banished the black beans and beef. She'd gone without food for days during her SPEAR training. Besides, she could stand to shed a few pounds. "It'll be dark in three or four hours. I can last that long."

"We'll have to stop well before dark," Carlos remarked, resuming the steady pace he'd set since they'd begun their trek. "We need to set up camp and find food before the light goes."

His mention of setting up camp brought the minor problem Margarita had been pushing to the back of her mind all afternoon slamming to the forefront. Given their erratic passage, they'd have to spend at least one night in the jungle. More likely two. Or three.

On the ground.

Under a mosquito net.

Together.

As much as she'd like to believe otherwise, the sudden clenching low in her stomach had nothing to do with hunger. Not the kind that demanded black beans and beef, anyway. She was so caught up in the image of that single mosquito net that she didn't notice Carlos had frozen in his tracks until she almost tripped over him.

"What's the—"

"Get back!"

The command came out low, almost strangled. Her nerves shooting straight to red alert, Margarita swept the murky gloom ahead with a startled glance. Aside from the flash of a brilliant turquoise parrot swooping through the trees, nothing moved.

She dropped her voice to a whispery croak. "What is it? What do you see?"

"Get back!"

Slowly, so slowly, she inched backward.

Slowly, so slowly, Carlos reached down to un-snap the holster of his Beretta.

He whipped the weapon out at the precise instant a long, ratlike fanged creature dropped from a low-hanging branch to dangle almost in his face.

Chapter 5

It was a slug rat.

Margarita identified the repulsive creature a half second before Carlos blew it away. A distant cousin of the rats that infested Madrileño's cities, this jungle denizen possessed a foot-long, weasel-like body, rapacious fangs and claws sharp enough to tear apart the dead carcasses it fed on.

Although slug rats normally feasted on rotting flesh, the vicious rodents had been known to attack live chickens, pigs and even small children. After a baby had been gnawed almost to death last year, the government had instituted a bounty for each hide the farmers turned in.

Carlos might not need the bounty money, but he had no more love for the slimy predator than the rest of his countrymen. His first shot blasted it clear off the tree branch. He followed up with several whacking chops of the machete, then kicked the mangled remains into the gloom.

"Hey!" Margarita rushed forward, her stomach yowling a protest. "Why did you do that? He could have been our dinner!"

"We'll find something else."

"But…"

"We'll find something else!"

She skidded to a halt, her temper firing at the curt tone. She was all set to rip into him when she noticed the white lines bracketing his mouth. *And* the shudder that shook his muscled frame when he knelt to swipe the machete on a clump of moss.

Well, well, well. Big, strong, unshakable Carlos didn't like slug rats. Margarita didn't particularly care for them herself, but realizing his armor had this tiny chink in it suddenly put him in a different light. What a relief to learn he was human after all!

Feeling oddly lighthearted for someone who'd had a gun rammed into the underside of her chin, tumbled down a mountainside and trudged for hours through a steamy jungle, she squished along in his wake. Just when she thought she'd used up

even her considerable endurance, Carlos called a
halt beside a rock-strewn river. He cast a calculat-
ing eye on the rays slanting through the opening
cut by the rushing water.

"We've got about an hour until night drops,"
he announced, unhooking his vest.

Drops was the right word, she knew. There was
no twilight in the jungle. For reasons totally beyond her, day plunged into night almost in the
blink of an eye.

To her relief, Carlos set the matter of food as
his first priority. He tipped his head back to search
the smaller trees that had sprung up beside the
river, away from the smothering shadows of the
giant strangler figs. The plant growth was denser
in the narrow slice of sunlight that followed the
riverbed, and the vegetation far more varied.

"I see some plantains in that tree," he said with
a note of satisfaction. "I'll climb up and cut
enough for supper and breakfast. Think you can
collect some of those ferns to make a bed and figure out how to rig the mosquito net over a low-
hanging limb?"

"I'll give it my best shot," she replied dryly.

It didn't escape her attention that he automati-
cally assumed the role of provider, assigning her
the duties of hearth tender. That was fine with Margarita. Let him hunt and gather. She'd piddle

around with the ferns. She could assert herself quickly enough if and when it became necessary.

Carlos unholstered his weapon and placed it on a boulder close to the river's edge. "I'll leave the Beretta with you. Just in case."

"There might be rats in that tree," she reminded him. "Won't you need it?"

Another shudder rippled the muscles under his black T-shirt. "I'll take the machete."

"But…"

"I'm not leaving you unprotected. But be careful with the gun. It doesn't have a safety. You just point and shoot."

"Got it," she snapped, struggling with the contradictory emotions his protectiveness always raised in her.

Carlos took another look at the fruit dangling high above his head. With a little grunt, he planted his boots against the scaly bark and started walking up the trunk.

Margarita watched his ascent for several moments, riveted despite herself by the play of muscle under his ragged T-shirt. Strange. Why hadn't she ever noticed the raw power in those wide shoulders and mud-streaked arms before?

Probably because she'd only seen them covered in expertly tailored serge wool. Clingy black cotton altered the image considerably. Frowning, Margarita set about tearing feathery branches from ferns almost as tall as she was. She'd gathered one armful and was working on the second when a small crunch sounded above the river's tumble and fall.

She whirled. Her gaze flew upward first, searching for Carlos, then to the tangle of fallen tree limbs and dense growth along the riverbank.

Another crunch lifted the hairs on the back of her neck. Whoever or whatever was making its way through the underbrush moved heavy on its feet. The image of a scarred face leaped instantly into her mind. Dumping her armload of ferns, Margarita whipped over to the boulder where she'd laid the Beretta.

She didn't dare call to Carlos for fear of alerting the stalker in the undergrowth. Her heart pounding, she decided on a flanking maneuver. Moving silently on the springy earth, she melted into the ferns.

A moment later, a sharp crack split the air.

The shot caught Carlos just starting down, a stalk of green plantains dangling from a vine looped over his shoulder. Instant pandemonium erupted above him as parrots and toucans and quetzals burst from the branches, wings flapping. Monkeys screeched and took flight.

Carlos reacted instinctively. With the sound of the shot still reverberating through the jungle, he swept the area below him for signs of Margarita, kicked away from the tree trunk and swung with a skill Tarzan might have admired toward the dense undergrowth. He released the vine at the bottom of its arc, dropped a good twenty feet and hit the spongy ground running. Silent as a shadow, he knifed through the undergrowth with murder in his heart. If anything or anyone had harmed Margarita...

The sight of her denim-covered backside stopped him cold. She was facing away from him, bent almost double as she dragged something through the brush. His heart still pumping pure stimulant, Carlos searched the area beyond her for possible dangers. Nothing moved in the shadowy green...except Margarita. Grunting and wiggling, she backed toward him.

She didn't appear to be under duress, but until he knew exactly who'd fired that shot and what the hell she was dragging through the brush, he wasn't taking any chances. He called to her, his voice low and urgent.

"Margarita! What is it?"

Twisting her upper body, she aimed a grin over her shoulder. "Dinner."

"What!"

She straightened, puffing. Only then did he see the furry gray carcass of a javelina at her feet.

"I heard him in the brush and went to investigate," she said with a cheerful unconcern that had Carlos grinding his jaw. A dozen different scenarios had flashed through his head during his wild swing on that vine. None of them included a grinning, tousle-haired huntress bagging a wild pig for supper.

"I don't know who was more startled when we came face-to-face," she confessed, laughter dancing in her violet eyes. "But when he charged, I decided I wasn't going to argue with those tusks."

The spearlike canines protruded a good five inches. Observing their razor-sharp tips, Carlos felt sweat pool at the small of his back.

"*Dios!* Did you bring him down with a single shot?"

"I got lucky," she said with a modesty belied by her smug expression. Bending, she grabbed a hind leg. "Help me haul him back to camp. Then you can cook our supper while I wash up."

Despite the blood still thundering through his veins, he couldn't miss the cocky note of command. His brow hooked, but he didn't argue. She'd made the kill. It was only fair that he clean and cook it.

An hour and a half later, Margarita licked a dollop of grease from her fingers. For the tenth time in as many minutes, her eyes strayed from the man across the fire toward the mosquito net draped from a low-hanging tree branch.

Just the sight of that small white tent was enough to make her pulse flutter. Resolutely, she pulled her gaze away from the net and forced herself to concentrate on the present instead of the future that loomed closer with every passing moment.

Really, all things considered, they'd done pretty well so far. For the first time since that plunge down the mountainside, they were both full and relatively safe. Margarita's stomach rumbled contentedly as it digested roast pork and stringy plantains baked with the wild berries that had given them a sweet, tart flavor, all washed down by clear water.

Beyond the radius of the little fire Carlos had so carefully built, inky blackness blanketed the jungle. Unless Simon and his cohorts possessed highly sophisticated night-vision equipment and extraordinary tracking ability, they couldn't possibly follow a trail at night.

Nor could anyone else, Carlos's men included.

A single glance was enough to see that uncertainty about the fate of the squad chafed at its leader. He'd spoken little while he worked his way through his meal. Once or twice, she'd caught him frowning as he searched the blackness outside the small circle of firelight.

It was an eerie, pulsing sort of darkness. Strange green objects flickered against the black velvet backdrop. Fireflies and beetles, Margarita supposed. Some object she chose not to examine too closely glowed almost phosphorescent a short distance away.

"How many of your men came with you?" she asked, breaking into his thoughts.

He glanced up, his face cast in different shades of gold by the tiny, glowing fire. "Eleven, including Lieutenant Carreras."

"Miguel?"

A hollow feeling curled around her heart. The vicious exchange of gunfire she'd heard right before she plowed through the vines at the mouth of the cave indicated the squad had run into trouble. Big trouble. Pray God, Miguel and the others survived. She liked the stocky, taciturn officer who served as Carlos's aide. Moreover, she sympathized with his undeclared love for her flighty young cousin.

A sudden image of Anna laughing at her partner as they floated to the strains of the "Blue Danube" formed in her mind. Was it only last night Margarita had watched from the shadows of the balcony while her cousin flirted with Carlos? It seemed like another lifetime!

A flicker of irritation accompanied the memory. It wasn't jealousy. How could she be jealous because her cousin gazed so adoringly into the face of the man Margarita had refused repeatedly to marry? Yet that inexplicable niggle of annoyance prompted an observation.

"Miguel's in love with Anna."

Still preoccupied with his thoughts, Carlos nodded. "I know."

"But she, I think, fancies herself in love with you."

That got his attention. Lifting his head, he studied her enigmatically through the heat waves shimmering above the fire.

"Does Anna's infatuation bother you, *querida?*"

"Not at all," she lied. "Does it bother you?"

He parried the question with consummate diplomacy. "The attentions of such a beautiful young woman must flatter any man."

"Spoken like a true politician. No wonder my uncle is so anxious to have you stand for the vacant senate seat. Are you going to do it?" she asked, as much to delay the inevitable as to hear his answer.

"I haven't decided. My background is in the

military. It's what I know. What I love. I think I can do more good at the Ministry of Defense, but..."

His glance met hers. She knew without being told what he was thinking. Her uncle hoped to fill the seat vacated by a member of the opposition caught taking bribes with someone he could trust. Someone who would support his programs. Someone related to him by ties of marriage.

"Is it a package deal, Carlos? Am I supposed to come with that senate seat?"

His mouth kicked up. "If I thought your uncle could deliver on a deal like that, I would have already declared my candidacy."

That wasn't exactly what Margarita wanted to hear. It didn't help that she wasn't sure what she *did* want to hear. Certainly not the words he uttered next.

"We'd better get some sleep. I want to travel at first light tomorrow."

Her pulse hitched again, harder this time. Her voice cool, she suggested an alternative arrangement. "Shouldn't we take turns keeping watch?"

"I sleep lightly," he answered with a shrug. "The frogs and other night creatures will give sufficient warning if someone approaches."

She had only to tune into the cacophony around her to know the truth of his observation. Now that their initial alarm had passed, the denizens of the jungle seemed to have accepted her and Carlos into their midst. The air vibrated with whistles and whoops and chirps. Bats whooshed through the trees. Night-feeding reptiles crunched with clearly audible delight on their prey. Margarita didn't doubt all these creatures would go deadly quiet, then burst into a frenzy of flight should new predators intrude on the scene.

"Just to be safe," Carlos added with offhanded nonchalance, "I rigged a few perimeter defenses while you were at the river."

"Like what?"

His smile didn't bode well for any unexpected late-night visitors. "Let's just say I sharpened a few more stakes than we needed to roast your javelina."

She had to admit a grudging admiration. The man certainly knew his way around a jungle. She was thinking about the extraordinary skills he'd displayed today when he stood and stretched like a lazy, replete panther.

Instantly, her mind emptied of everything but the hard planes and muscled curves displayed in such tantalizing detail by the firelight. Damn that black T-shirt, anyway. It left nothing to the imagination…and everything!

"I'm going to wash the mud off my face and

arms,'' he told her. ''I'll bank the fire and join you under the netting when I'm through.''

The casual promise scraped on her nerves. Frowning, she watched him melt into the darkness beyond the meager light thrown by the campfire. When her gaze shifted from the spot where the jungle had swallowed him whole to the white drape hanging from its tree limb, the hitch in her pulse drummed into an erratic beat.

Oh, for pity's sake! How absurd to tremble like a nervous virgin at the mere thought of sharing a few square inches of bed space. As much as he'd disconcerted her this morning with that savage kiss, Carlos was still…Carlos. Rock solid. Dependable. Honorable. He wouldn't demand more of her than she wanted to give.

Or would he?

Yesterday, she would have laughed at the idea. Tonight, the oddest prickle of uncertainty hounded her as she cleaned the campsite. This Carlos bore only a passing resemblance to the man who'd courted her with suave finesse. The jungle had stripped away his sophisticated layers, baring a hard-edged stranger beneath.

He stirred her in ways the other Carlos hadn't. She was honest enough to admit that. He also made her just a little nervous. The deputy defense minister she could control. She couldn't shake the feeling that no one could control this bronzed jungle warrior.

The unsettling thought needled her as she completed the clean-up chores. There weren't many to complete. They'd already wrapped and safely stashed the leftover cooked meat they'd carry with them tomorrow. A quick toss disposed of the leaves they'd used as bowls. That basic task accomplished, Margarita crossed to the netting hung from a low branch.

Her heart thudding, she took off her boots and set them beside the mound of ferns, then crawled under the net and found a comfortable position on the leafy bed. The useful nylon vest made a lumpy pillow. The plastic water sack, unneeded with the river so close, protected her back and hips from the damp earth.

But nothing could protect her from the tiny shocks that jolted through her when Carlos lifted the net and stretched out beside her. She held herself stiffly while he draped the netting to his satisfaction and rolled into her, his front to her back. Hooking an arm over her waist, he spooned her body into his. Or tried to. Her rigid back refused to bend to his contours.

''Relax.''

Uh-huh! As if she could relax with his breath warm on her cheek and her bottom planted squarely in the cradle of his thighs. She stared unblinking at the fire's dim glow, her breath almost completely suspended. With every rise and fall of his chest against her spine, her senses inched closer to maximum overload.

Each twitch of his muscles set her nerves screaming. His clean, river-washed scent formed such a contrast to the jungle's dank earthiness that Margarita drank it in hungrily. Too hungrily. Distracted by the sensations crowding in on her, she gave a little start when his voice sounded low and husky in her ear.

"I'm not going to rip off your clothes and make love to you, if that's what has you so worried."

Wondering if he thought she would have nothing to say in the matter should he try, Margarita twisted in his arms.

"I'm not worried," she replied with a slight stretch of the truth. "But, just out of curiosity—why not?"

Ferns rustled as he propped himself on one elbow. He loomed over her, his cheeks and chin shadowed by a day's growth of stubble. Black eyes reflecting tiny pinpoints of light from the banked fire held hers.

"When I make love to you—"

"*When?*"

White teeth flashed in a smile. "Make no mis-

take, I will make love to you. But not on the
ground, like animals, and not with one ear tuned
to every whistle and hoot in the jungle.''

There it was again. His iron control. Even here,
in a spot so wild and remote it might never have
seen the passage of other humans, he could still
clamp a tight rein on the primitive side of his nature she'd glimpsed so briefly this morning.

Damn the man! He made her head swim with
these switches in personality.

''You're very sure of yourself,'' she replied with
a touch of acid.

''Yes, I am.''

Her nails cut half-circles in her palms. A totally
perverse need to prick his bubble of masculine
complacency gripped her.

''What if I told you *I've* been lying here thinking
about ripping off your clothes?''

''Have you?''

She made no effort to dodge the truth this time.
She could hardly breathe for the constriction in her
throat. Her nerves sizzled at every point they
touched. Hip against hip. Thigh under thigh. Breast
to chest.

''Yes.''

At her blunt admission, his smile slipped, then
disappeared completely.

Margarita stared at him, her heart leaping at the

sudden, sharp cut to his features. For several seconds she considered following up on her frank acknowledgment of the desire arcing between them. She needed only to lift her hands a couple of inches. Edge them under his T-shirt. Feast on that glorious combination of warm skin and hard muscle for a moment or two, then slide her palms down to harder, hotter regions. Before she could act on the insane impulse, he bent his head.

"Not on the ground," he murmured, brushing her mouth with his. "Not like animals. But soon, *mi amor*. Soon."

Chapter 6

Carlos had spent more than a few uncomfortable nights in his lifetime. During his years in uniform, he'd bivouacked on sand so hot it blistered his skin through his clothes and laid his bedroll atop cold, sucking mud. Often, he'd stretched out on bare tarmac while he waited for airlift to the latest crisis spot. Once, he'd passed forty-eight hours wedged in the crook of a tree fifty feet above the ground, a dirty scrap of cloth knotted around the bullet hole in his thigh while he monitored the activities of the murderous band of terrorists camped below. But as he cradled Margarita in his arms and waited for sleep to claim her, he suspected this night would top his never-do-this-again list.

Gradually, she relaxed. Slowly, her rigidity gave way to exhaustion. She twitched a couple of times and muttered once or twice as she slipped into a doze. Finally, she lay soft and pliant in his arms.

In direct contrast, Carlos hurt more with each passing moment. He couldn't breathe without drawing in her earthy combination of river-washed hair and smoke-scented skin. With every brush of her breasts against his arm, he felt his jaw tighten another notch. When she gave a little grunt and wiggled her bottom into his groin, he ground his teeth and cursed himself for a fool.

He could have had her. When she'd wedged herself around to face him, looked him square in the eye and admitted bluntly that she'd been thinking about ripping off his clothes, he'd almost lost what little remained of his control.

Dios! Did she think he was made of stone? Didn't she guess that he ached all over with wanting her? Every muscle in his body crawled with a need so raw it consumed him. Despite his fine speech of a few minutes ago, he was only a breath away from rolling her over, dragging down her jeans and thrusting into her smooth, slick depths. Right here. On the leafy earth. Like animals. Grunting. Grinding. Each losing themselves in the fury of the moment.

Only his gut-level need to protect the woman he

now thought of as his own held him back. He was damned if he'd make love to Margarita for the first time with one ear tuned to the sounds of the jungle for possible danger. He couldn't risk her life by letting down his guard even for a moment. What's more, he suspected that one frantic joining wouldn't be enough for either of them. When the dam finally burst, the resulting flood would sweep them both away. Carlos fully intended to get them both to high, safe ground before that happened.

Gritty-eyed with fatigue, he eased onto his back, brought Margarita around to curl against his chest and stared at the unrelenting darkness.

Morning, like night, came suddenly in the jungle. There was a brief graying when blackness shadowed into dim shapes. Seemingly within the next heartbeat, gray turned luminous and green.

With Margarita's head heavy on his shoulder, Carlos listened to the sounds of the jungle coming awake. Toucans cawed. Hummingbirds whizzed by. Mosquitoes buzzed. By far the most fearsome of the new day's sounds came from the howler monkeys as they announced the dawn. Deep-throated roars produced by their giant voice boxes and amplified by a hollow bone at the base of their tongue warned other troops away from their territory. Their calls echoed like thunder in the distance.

When a nearby howler let loose a hoarse cry not far from the campsite, Margarita stirred but didn't wake. Carlos let her sleep as long as he dared, watching the dew drip from the moss fuzzing the tree branches above them and run in streaks down the netting. He tracked several silvery drops all the way to the ground before he nudged her gently.

"Rita."

She made a noise halfway between a grunt and a groan. He prodded her again.

"It's dawn."

"Mmm."

"We should move out."

"Give me a minute," she mumbled.

Her minute spun into two, then five. Carlos shifted an arm deadened by her weight. Grumbling, she rolled tight against him and burrowed her nose into his shoulder.

"I'm getting the idea you're not a morning person," he drawled.

She sniffed and muttered into his T-shirt. "Until I down some caffeine, I'm not any kind of a person."

"I'll remember that."

The promise buried in his reply brought her head

up. Blinking owlishly, she treated him to a cranky stare.

"Just for the record, I'm not real good at sexual repartee first thing in the morning."

"I'll remember that, too."

She was still frowning when he lifted the netting and tipped his boots upside down to dislodge any uninvited night visitors.

"I'm going to the river to wash up. I'll leave the Beretta with you. Try to avoid any more up close encounters with javelinas," he added in his driest voice.

"I'll stay out of their way if they stay out of mine."

He left her sitting cross-legged on the leafy bed, dragging her fingers through her hair and squinting at the murky green dawn with unfriendly eyes.

Although he didn't show it, Carlos didn't feel particularly friendly himself. The long hours with Margarita's body curled tight against his had put a few painful kinks in his muscles, some of which he suspected might remain there permanently. Rolling his neck and shoulders, he made his way to the tumbling, rock-strewn river and stripped off.

Repeated dunkings in the clear, cool river helped loosen the knots. So did a brisk rubdown with a handful of scratchy leaves from a handy *Inga* tree. His skin tingling, he pulled on his clothes and combed his clean hair with his fingers before retracing his steps. He was greeted by the sight of Margarita sitting beside the smoldering fire, her hands busy as she plaited vines together.

Madre de Dios! How could the woman look even more delectable in his scruffy fatigue shirt than she had in flame-colored silk?

"I've made a backpack," she informed him, holding up a loosely woven pouch of leaves. "We can carry enough of the roasted meat to last a day or two."

Her ingenuity impressed him. So did the tangy, sweet scent that drifted from the fire. She followed his gaze, smiling when his stomach gave a loud rumble.

"I baked the rest of the bananas and berries for breakfast."

"So I see."

She poked at the leaf-wrapped bundles with a small stick. "I also found some wild mangoes when I was gathering vines. You can chow down while I wash up."

The muscles Carlos had just worked loose jerked into knots again. Sternly, he clamped down on an offer to perform back-scrubbing services for her.

"Don't take too long. We need to get moving."

"No, sir!"

"I'll put some fresh antiseptic ointment on your wrists when you finish."

"Yes, sir!"

Flipping him a cocky, two-fingered salute, she strolled down the trail to the riverbank. A smile played at Carlos's mouth as he squatted and devoured his breakfast of wild fruit salad.

Any inclination to smile disappeared very soon after they set out again. Leaving the river behind, they were forced to capture their drinking water in the plastic pouch during the frequent thunderstorms. The pouch sloshed awkwardly against Carlos's thigh with each step, adding its weight to that of his vest. Margarita carried her handmade backpack slung over her shoulders by the plaited vines. She also took possession of the Beretta while Carlos swung the machete to cut a swath through the dangling strangler roots and towering ferns.

Within minutes, their shirts were plastered to their backs. Within hours, they'd used up the energy generated by the night's rest and were drawing on their reserves. It was impossible to follow a straight path. Cliffs thrust out of the jungle like granite walls. Ravines cut savage gashes in the earth's surface, necessitating long, leg-cramping detours. Knees scraping, palms raw from grasping vines, they slithered down one steep bank, then dragged themselves up the next.

Storms crashed and boomed intermittently overhead. Torrential rains bulleted through the canopy, adding to their misery. Margarita soon lost all sense of time and direction. Hot, dank air cut through her lungs in jagged pants when Carlos blew out a long breath and finally signaled a rest break.

She thought it was mid-afternoon. It had to be mid-afternoon. The dense green umbrella overhead let in only a few rays of light, but she felt as though she'd been swatting mosquitoes and slogging through greenery for days, if not weeks.

"How far have we come?"

He pulled the Global Positioning Satellite directional finder from the sleeveless vest and squinted at it through lashes beaded with sweat. "A little over five miles."

Her jaw sagged. "You're kidding, right?"

"Unfortunately, I'm not."

"Are you sure you know how to read that thing?"

He didn't bother to reply.

That meant the village was still a good five miles distant. Swallowing her dismay, Margarita sank onto a fallen log and placed the Beretta beside her. Her aching shoulders cried for a break.

His eyes unreadable behind those ridiculously thick black lashes, Carlos searched her face. "Can you make it?"

"I can make it."

"You've surprised me these past two days at how well you kept up."

Margarita accepted the implied compliment with a nod and a private little smirk.

"You're in better shape than I realized," he remarked casually.

Too casually. She caught the question behind his comment and felt her bubble of smug pride burst. Warily, she eased out of the backpack.

"I try to exercise regularly."

"When?"

"Excuse me?"

Planting a boot on the log, he hooked an elbow on his knee and regarded her thoughtfully.

"When do you exercise, Rita? I know you're usually at work before anyone else arrives, and you've certainly used the excuse of working late often enough to avoid having dinner with me. So how did you develop the stamina for the march we just put in, and how do you maintain it?"

"I do Jazzercise at home in the evenings," she replied, reaching up to rub her aching shoulders. "It helps me relax."

The brutal workout she put herself through every

night was about as relaxing as sleeping on a bed of rusty nails. Her personal habits were her business, however, and no one else's—as she would have pointed out if Carlos hadn't brushed her hands aside at that moment and taken over the task of kneading her shoulders. After their initial shock of protest, her aching muscles melted under the magic of his strong, sure hands.

"You escape a brutal kidnapper, take down a wild pig with a single shot and trek for two days through the jungle without a single complaint," he mused. "I don't know many women who could accomplish any one of those feats, let alone all three."

"Mmm."

"Men, either."

She didn't care for the direction of this conversation, but his incredible hands proved too distracting for more than a flippant response.

"Desperation is a great motivator. I've surprised myself, too."

"Have you?"

"Yes, I— Oh! Oh, God! Do that again."

Rotating his thumbs in the gap between her shoulder blades, he massaged the knotted tendons. Margarita closed her eyes and mewled in delight.

Diabolically, he waited until she was swimming in mindless pleasure before he slid his hands around her neck, hooked his thumbs under her jaw and tilted her head back against his knee.

"Do you take me for a fool, Rita?"

The question brought her lids flying open. Shock jolted through her when she saw the suppressed fury in his dark eyes.

"Tell me what game you're playing," he growled.

She wanted to. At that moment, with her head captured in his hands and his whisker-roughened chin set at a dangerous angle only inches above her, she wanted to tell him about SPEAR, about the call from Marcus Waters that had sent her rushing to the prison, about the scar-faced Simon and his seemingly murderous vendetta against Jonah.

Silently cursing the vow of secrecy she'd made so many years ago, she fell back on the same ambiguous answer she'd given Carlos before.

"I'm not playing any kind of a game."

Something flickered behind the anger in his eyes before they went cold and flat. Frustration, she thought. Or was it hurt that she wouldn't trust him with the truth?

Abruptly, he released her. "Are you rested enough to move out?"

"Carlos…"

"We should be able to cover another half mile before dark."

He picked up the machete and swung away. Feeling miserable, and annoyed because of it, Margarita slid her arms through the woven shoulder straps, tucked the Beretta into the waistband of her jeans and followed.

Their second night in the jungle passed much as the first had.

They shared a meal of cold roast pig and wild avocados, washed up with water from the plastic pouch and crawled under the mosquito net. Margarita lay cocooned against Carlos, all too aware of the distance between them despite the intimacy of their embrace. She ached to twist around in his arms, take his cheeks in her palms and kiss away the coldness that had settled in his eyes. The intensity of the need kept her from sleep, despite the exhaustion that pulled at her like a tide.

It also confused the heck out of her. She'd never felt this urge to pet and soothe and coax Carlos before. Nor had he ever withdrawn from her so deliberately. Only now did she realize how much she'd taken his even temperament and constant, if occasionally annoying, attentions for granted.

Ruefully, she recalled her mother's often repeated maxim that no wife should ever go to sleep angry with her husband unless she wanted to wake up angry with him, as well. Since the still beautiful

Maria de las Fuentes had ruled supreme over her husband in all matters relating to her household for more than thirty years, Margarita conceded that her mother might have a point.

If only it was that simple, she thought, shifting restlessly on the nest of ferns. If only she could accept the role of a proper Madrileñan wife, content to keep busy at home while Carlos provided for her and the children she one day hoped to have.

Without warning, her womb clenched. The idea of bearing children, *his* children, gripped her and wouldn't let go. She stared into the darkness, envisioning the offspring she and Carlos would produce. Grinning, mischievous little girls. Cocky, dark-eyed boys who'd swagger along in their father's footsteps. One baby every other year, she thought wryly. Like a proper Madrileñan wife.

To her disgust, the prospect didn't dismay her as much as it usually did. Quite the contrary, in fact. An unexpected longing to hold Carlos's child to her breast tugged at something deep inside her. Would it be so bad to lose her identity in marriage and family? To spend her days at home and her nights in her husband's arms? Listening to his breath, warm and steady in her ear. Feeling his heartbeat strong and sure against her back.

For a few insidious moments, the prospect shimmered like a beacon in the darkness.

It was the jungle, she thought irritably. This damned jungle. The green, primordial rawness was closing in on her, stirring instincts older than time. To mate. To procreate. To sweep out a cave and build a nest. To soothe the disgruntled male who held her so stiffly in his arms.

The *very* disgruntled male, judging by the terse order he issued when she shifted restlessly once more.

"Go to sleep."

"I'm trying."

His arm tightened about her waist warningly. "Try harder."

The curt reply might have sparked a heated exchange if it wasn't so absurd—and if Margarita hadn't become suddenly aware of the reason he held her so stiffly, his body angled away from hers. All it took was another slight movement, a small, restless twitch of her hips that brought them into contact with his.

Her eyes popped wide open. She sucked in a swift breath, electrified by the rock-hard arousal pressed against her. Heat flared in her belly and burned its way into her chest.

Carlos jerked away from the intimate contact. In a voice that could have ground glass, he snarled in her ear.

"Go to sleep, dammit."

* * *

His disposition didn't improve with the dawn. Or with the passage of three more tortuous miles.

Grimly efficient, he whacked a trail through the dangling vines and ferns as tall as small trees. Margarita followed, even more confused than before by the contradictory feelings this man roused in her. She chafed at the shuttered expression in his eyes when they caught hers. Chafed more at the knowledge he wanted her every bit as much as she wanted him. She had only to remember the way he'd jutted against her jean-clad hip to go dry in the throat. Damn him and his iron control!

The consoling thought that he'd laid awake as long as she had last night kept her going for most of the day. They stopped only twice, once at midday to eat and once an hour or so before dusk. Sighing, Margarita eased off the backpack and rubbed the grooves cut in her shoulders by the plaited vine straps while Carlos scaled a jagged granite cliff to search for curls of smoke that would indicate the presence of humans. He found them, but not to the east in the direction of the village.

A muscle was ticking in the side of his jaw when he slid down the cliff face.

"They're behind us."

"The escaped prisoner and his band?"

"That's my guess. None of my men would be so foolish as to light a cook fire before nightfall."

"How far away are they?"

"A mile or more."

She sagged in disappointment. A mile in the jungle meant they were hours away. Too far to determine who, in fact, had built that fire. Her gut told her it was Simon, though, as Carlos had surmised.

The muscle in his jaw jumped again as he regarded her with dark, hooded eyes. "This man must want you very badly to track you like this."

Simon didn't want her, except as a means to get at the man at the helm of SPEAR.

"My guess is he wants us both," she countered, reaching for her backpack. "I told you, he blames you for destroying his base of operation in Madrileño. He's after you as much as me."

It was only half the truth, but it was better than a lie. Or so she told herself as she turned away.

"We'd better keep moving as long as we have light."

Slinging the pack over one shoulder, she was groping behind her for the other strap when the woven vine pouch thumped against her back. Startled, she halted with her arm in midair. The sensation of something slithering onto her shoulder stopped her heart.

She had time for a single prayer.

Let it be a small boa! Not a deadly pit viper or coral snake!

She caught a whiff of fetid breath, felt a brush of slimy fur. The realization that a slug rat had climbed onto her shoulder hit her at the precise instant close to two hundred pounds of fury slammed into her back.

Margarita pitched forward as Carlos ripped the uninvited hitchhiker off her neck.

Chapter 7

To a man who loathed the vicious rodents as much as Carlos, seeing one crawl onto Margarita's shoulder was like watching his worst nightmare played out in excruciating slow motion.

In the half second it took him to spear through the air, he registered a pointed snout, bared claws and a fanged mouth stretched in a hideous parody of a grin. Then his fist closed around the furry body and he went down, twisting in midair to avoid Margarita as she collapsed under his flying tackle.

Pure luck got him a one-handed grip behind the rat's head so it couldn't whip around and bite him. Pure adrenaline kept his right arm outstretched and

the vicious fangs a good foot from his face as he
rolled away from Margarita. He heard her panting
sob as she scrambled to her knees, but didn't—
couldn't—take his eyes from the hissing, spitting
rodent that slashed his neck and arms with its tail.

On his back, with the rat's fangs a rigid arm's
length straight above him, he fumbled with his left
hand for the machete tucked into its scabbard.

Crack!

The single shot split the air. The three inches of
rat protruding from Carlos's fist disintegrated.

He stared at his bunched fingers for a stunned
moment, not hearing the clamor that filled the air
as startled birds flapped into the sky and monkeys
screeched into flight. Then his face contorted and
he jerked upright, fighting free of the slack carcass.
He'd barely managed to fling it away when Margarita threw herself down on her knees beside him
and shoved him flat on his back.

"Lie still!" She followed her fierce command
with a swift visual search of his face and neck.
"Were you bitten?"

"No, I—"

"Don't move! Those things carry rabies."

"Never mind me. What about you?"

"I'm okay. Dammit, don't move."

Her eyes a purplish-black in their intensity, she

tore open his vest and checked his upper arms and shoulders.

"Did you feel a bite? Here? Here? Oh..." Her gaze locked on his left shoulder. "Dear God!"

Carlos swallowed.

"It's only a scrape," she said with a rush of relief, resuming her intent scrutiny. When she tugged at the hem of his T-shirt, Carlos decided he'd better call a halt before she stripped him down to the buff.

"I wasn't bitten." He snagged her wrists just above the bandages. "I caught the thing right behind the head. It couldn't get at me."

"Are you sure?"

"I'm sure."

Her throat still clogged with fear, Margarita stared at him. He hadn't been bitten. He was okay. It took several shattering moments for her mind to absorb those basic facts.

The instant it did, delayed reaction set in. A giant shudder racked her, starting in her upper torso and clawing its way downward. Another, even longer and harder than the first, followed. Her straining thighs quivered, then gave out completely. Plopping on her heels, she did something she hadn't done since she was a little girl.

She burst into tears.

Great, sloppy, gulping sobs that tore at her chest and throat.

"Rita." Alarm skittered across Carlos's face. "Don't cry. It's all right."

"No, it's not!"

Pulling a hand free, she pounded on his chest as though it was his fault the foot-long rat had decided to hitch a ride in her backpack.

"The thing might have had rabies. You might have died," she wailed, thumping his chest again. "Right here, before my eyes."

"*Dios!*" He snatched her wrist once more. "You just took off its head with a shot few marksmen could make and now you cry?"

"Don't talk about it! Don't talk at all. Just..." Tears streaming down her cheeks, she flung herself forward. "Just kiss me."

Still sobbing, she locked her mouth on his. It wasn't the neatest kiss Carlos had ever given or received. Noses bumped. Chins scraped. Her squirming body almost slithered off his chest. One knee came down between his thighs, a little to close to his groin for comfort.

With a grunt, he locked an arm around her waist and rolled them both over. The cumbersome vest she'd unclasped a few moments ago slid off his shoulder. Impatiently, he yanked free of it and they rolled again, legs tangling, mouths fused. She strained against him, her body hot and slick against his.

It was a wild mating of tongues and teeth and torsos. Carlos's mind emptied of every thought but Margarita, every sensation but Margarita. The curve of her waist under his hand. The tangle of rain-damp hair that whipped around them with every twisting turn.

He made a last attempt at sanity and tried to pull back. She wouldn't let him put so much as an inch between them.

Her hands frantic, she dragged his T-shirt up and over his head. Her mouth was hot on his skin, her teeth sharp as they scraped the corded muscles of his shoulder.

This wasn't what he wanted for her. The thought rifled through his mind even as he attacked the buttons of the oversize fatigue shirt she'd adopted as her own. Every civilized instinct in his body recoiled from taking her like this. On the ground. Rolling on the dank earth like frenzied beings. But when she wiggled her arms out of the shirt he'd all but ripped from her back, he needed only one glimpse of the scrap of red lace covering her breasts to know it, too, had to go.

Along with her jeans. And the tiny triangle of red beneath. When the denim and silk caught on her boots, trapping her legs together, Carlos had to fight the urge to whip out his machete and slash through the fabric.

His heart was slamming against his chest by the time he'd stripped her down to a wild mass of blue-black hair, a tiny oval locket and an expanse of skin so creamy and smooth his throat closed. The sight of her violet eyes dark with hunger and the tips of her breasts hardened to points fired a need so deep and savage he rolled away and surged to his feet.

"What are you doing?"

Dismay at his abrupt withdrawal blanked her face until his hands went to his belt. In less than a minute, he'd shed his clothing. All trappings of civilization went with them. He was on fire to mate with the woman sprawled naked on layers of green, her head back, her tangled hair sweeping the ground. Instinct made him place the Beretta and machete within easy reach atop their pile of clothing. An even deeper instinct brought him to stand beside her, giving her one last chance to retreat before he claimed her.

For a moment, only a moment, a tiny alarm sounded in the back of Margarita's mind. She almost cowered before the sun-bronzed warrior towering over her. The dim light did little to disguise the hard planes and contours of his body. Or the rigid shaft that jutted from the thatch of dark hair at his groin. Her throat went dry even as damp heat burned between her legs.

He looked so fierce. As though he wanted to warn her things were about to change irrevocably between them.

She didn't need a warning. She was all too aware that she and Carlos were about to cross an invisible line. What waited for them on the other side?

She couldn't guess, and at that moment couldn't summon the will to even try. All she wanted was to slide her palms over those corded muscles. To taste again his mouth on hers and feel him plunge into her with all the power of his magnificent body. Silencing the last tiny warning bell, she yielded to all that was feminine in her and curved her lips in deliberate invitation.

The invisible restraints holding Carlos snapped. With a growl, he sank to his knees. His fists wrapped around her ankles, spread her legs. The glitter in his eyes primed her more than any so-phisticated foreplay could ever have done. Her womb clenched. She was ready for him, so ready she ground out a sound that was part plea, part angry demand.

The strangled cry brought him surging forward. In one brutally swift, incredibly skilled move, he seated himself between her thighs, and thrust into her. With the first lunge, her hips slammed into the springy earth. With the second, her back arched.

Carlos used her body's leverage to diabolical advantage. Fisting his hands in her hair, he held her head and kept her hips canted at exactly the right angle for him to ram home with every flex of his thighs. Hoarse cries of pleasure ripped from the back of her throat, lost in the sounds that rose from his chest. Wrapping her legs around his lean flanks and her hands around the satiny steel of his arms, she matched him thrust for thrust.

Margarita had never known such blinding, shattering pleasure. It coiled at her core, pulsed outward like a strobe light gone berserk. Desperately, she tried to hold it back.

Not now! Not yet!

She didn't realize she'd moaned the words aloud until Carlos dragged up his head.

"Yes, now." He locked his thighs, filling her so completely she gasped. "Open your eyes, *querida.* I want to watch your pleasure take you."

He waited until she'd focused her spinning senses enough to see his face before he angled one hip and reached between their sweat-slick bodies. With his thumb and fingers exerting wicked pressure, he drew back, then slid into her again. And again.

Margarita almost crawled out of her skin. Her

nails dug into his arms. Her body heaved upward. Even then she might have held out for another moment or two if he hadn't contorted just enough to take one of her nipples in his mouth. Three days' growth of beard scraped against her tender skin. His teeth tortured the engorged tip of her breast.

"Carlos! In the name of— Oh!"

She arched, going taut as a drawn bow. White heat lanced into her belly.

In some distant corner of her mind, she thought she heard a howler monkey's hoarse, guttural cry. Shocked, she realized the animal scream had come from her. A half second later, she splintered into a thousand pieces.

With a savage sound that swallowed hers, Carlos flexed his thighs, plunged deep and rode the crest of her climax to his own.

"I'm sorry."

The husky apology dragged Margarita from her semi-stupor. Lifting heavy lids, she blinked at the whisker-roughened face mere inches from her own.

"Why?"

"I shouldn't have... I've never..." Disgust rippled over his features. "I've never lost control like that."

She didn't have the heart to tell him she would

have torn out his liver with her bare hands if he'd held back another moment.

"Did I hurt you, Rita?"

"No," she whispered, her voice still raw from the cries that had ripped from her throat.

He rolled off her, his body as taut as hers was limp. "The next time will be better."

Margarita's mind boggled at the thought. She couldn't imagine anything better. She was about to ask if he was serious when the sight of his tight buns trapped the words in her throat.

They were lean and muscular and only a shade less coppery than the rest of him. She was trying to imagine how he'd managed that all-over tan when he scooped up his clothes and shook them a couple times to dislodge any relatives of the now-deceased slug rat.

"The next time we make love, it will be in a bed," he promised grimly, yanking on his pants.

That warning bell in Margarita's mind started pinging again. She hadn't even recovered from this cataclysmic encounter and already he was talking about the next. Disconcerted, she reached for the fatigue shirt and shoved her arms into the sleeves.

"We'll take it slow," he vowed as he tugged on his black T-shirt. "So slow and sweet you'll want to die of it."

"I came pretty close to rigor mortis this time."

He didn't appear to appreciate her flippancy. If anything, the tight cast to his face grew more pronounced as he pulled on his socks and boots.

"Let's not get ahead of ourselves here," she said with what she hoped was a bright smile. She pushed to her feet, determined to defuse what was becoming a decidedly awkward moment. "We still have several miles of jungle to get through before we talk about what happens when we're out of it."

He shot her a swift look. Her stomach sinking, Margarita saw centuries of proud Madrileñan male in the rigid set of his jaw.

"I'm not some penniless cane cutter or rummed-up sailor off a foreign ship. I won't rut with you in the dirt, hitch up my pants and go contentedly on my way."

"Oh, for heaven's sake!" Exasperated, she raked a hand through her tangled hair. "This *is* the twenty-first century, you know. We don't have to set up housekeeping together just because we made love once."

"Once?" Cool, sophisticated Carlos made a distinctly rude sound. "If you think either of us will stop at once, you're even more rattled than I am at this point."

He had that right. From the moment that rat had crawled onto her shoulder, Margarita had plunged from one wild emotion to another. Fear for herself.

Terror for Carlos. Joyous relief. Searing lust. And
something deeper, something she couldn't define
yet, even to herself. She needed time to sort
through the tumult. Time to understand why the
prospect of sharing a bed and a house with Carlos
raised shivers all up and down her spine.

"This conversation is getting us nowhere," she
announced. She scooped up her panties, gave them
a cautionary shake, then waited for Carlos to turn
away so she could dress.

To her consternation, he refused to take the hint.
When she hesitated, his grin held just enough of a
mocking edge to grate on her nerves.

"As you pointed out, this *is* the twenty-first century."

His sardonic reminder brought a flush to her
cheeks, which warmed even more when Carlos let
his gaze drift from the bits of moss decorating her
hair to the gaping front of her shirt.

How ludicrous! Not ten minutes ago, they had
fused in the most elemental way a man and woman
can. Why in heaven's name did she now feel so
suddenly, absurdly shy?

Only after she'd fumbled the shirt buttons into
the holes did Margarita appreciate that stripping
down in the heat of passion was one thing. Putting
her clothes on while being watched by the man

who'd just taken her apart, nerve by nerve, kiss by kiss, was something else again.

Nor did it help her composure when he lifted a smug, all too knowing brow. "Some things don't change much over time, do they?"

With that obscure and thoroughly maddening remark, he gathered his vest and the machete and strolled far enough away to afford her an illusion of privacy.

But not so far that she didn't catch the way his head whipped around when a raucous screech sounded in the distance. The not-very-distant distance.

Another screech followed the first. In the next instant, a clamorous din assaulted her ears as flocks of startled birds flapped through the trees. With a low curse, Carlos dragged on his vest and threw a low, urgent command over his shoulder.

"Get your boots on!"

As if she needed the spur.

She was stamping them on when a flurry of movement shook the branches high above her. Craning her neck, Margarita spotted a dozen or so small, white-faced creatures flying through the trees.

Spider monkeys. A whole troop of them. In frantic flight. Something must have alerted them to danger. Her heart thumping, she grabbed her other boot. She had it half laced when Carlos crouched at her side. Swiftly, he placed the Beretta and two spare ammo clips on the ground beside her, then plowed his hand through the layers of vegetation. It came up oozing black mud.

"I'm going back."

She nodded, her fingers tugging frantically at the tangled laces.

"I'll leave the automatic with you." A flash of white teeth showed through the streaks of mud. "Just make sure you don't put a bullet between my eyes by mistake when I come back."

"If I put a bullet between your eyes, it won't be by mistake."

With swift efficiency, she ejected the magazine, checked its load and slapped it into place. Scooping up the spare clips, she scrambled to her feet.

"Let's go."

The brief grin snapped off his face. "You're not going anywhere."

Giving that bit of idiocy the total lack of response it deserved, she squinted upward. Hazy light filtered through the trees at a decided angle.

"We've got another half hour of light, maybe less. Since you're the one with the night-vision goggles, you'd better take the point."

"Dammit, I don't have time to argue with you."

"Who's arguing? Move out, *commandante*."

Carlos took one look at her face and realized his choices had narrowed to moving out as instructed or clipping her on the jaw and leaving her unconscious body hidden behind a rotting log.

She read his mind with unerring accuracy. "Don't even think about it," she warned softly. "I've got the gun, remember?"

He hesitated only another moment, then lifted his hand and swiped the remaining mud across her forehead and down her cheeks. Grimacing, she spit out the bits that oozed into her mouth.

His eyes were grim as he swung around to the trail he'd hacked through the vines what now seemed like hours ago.

"Stay to the left of the trail and at least twenty yards to the rear. I'll take the right. Listen for my signal." He pushed air through his teeth in a dry, chirpy rattle. "If you hear that call, get facedown in the mud and stay there unless I call for backup."

Margarita nodded. She might not have spent her years with SPEAR as a field operative, but she'd trained with some of the best agents in the business and knew the value of teamwork in situations like this. She wasn't going to jeopardize Carlos's life or her own with uncoordinated or unnecessary heroics.

He kissed her, hard, then melted into the darkening green beside the trail. She took the other side, the Beretta cocked and ready. Keeping low, she moved as silently as possible. She could only sense Carlos ahead of her, a stealthy presence in the gloom. Her ears strained to pick up the rustle of leaves. Her eyes searched for the slightest movement of tall, feathery ferns.

She had no idea how far they backtracked. Fifty tortuous yards. Seventy-five at most. She had just swiped the sweat from her eyes when she heard a swift, rattling chirp.

Margarita dropped like a stone.

Chapter 8

Margarita sprawled facedown in the dank vegetation, every sense on full alert. Her heart hammering, she kept herself immobile for what seemed
like forever. So long, in fact, a tiny orange frog
poked its head out of a clump of moss just inches
away and regarded her with wide-eyed curiosity.

Aside from the fearless little amphibian, she
might have been alone in the jungle. Utter silence
surrounded her. No insects whirred. No bats or
birds swooped. Not a good sign, she thought. Not
good at all.

At any moment she expected to hear shouts or
the rattle of gunfire. Her nerves stretched taut, she

was just sliding a hand down to her jeans pocket to make sure the spare ammo clips were easily accessible when a totally unexpected sound drifted through the moisture-laden air.

Laughter. Hearty male laughter.

She blinked. The frog blinked back.

Another deep chortle sent her mind leaping joyously. The squad! Miguel Carreras and the rest of the platoon must have been the ones following their trail. Relief pouring through her, Margarita dug her elbows into the earth and scrambled up. Her jerky movement sent the little orange frog diving for cover.

"It's all right, Rita," Carlos called as she gained her feet.

She pushed past a tangle of vines onto the path, expecting to see the short, stocky lieutenant. Instead, her startled gaze took in a walking cadaver.

The tall, incredibly gaunt stranger sported a battered straw hat, a monstrous pair of drooping gray mustachios and the baggy white cotton shirt and trousers worn by most Madrileñans. Sweeping off his hat, he whistled through the gap made by his missing front teeth.

"Ay. Your woman is most beautiful, *comandante.*"

"Yes, she is."

Ignoring Margarita's hiked brow, Carlos performed the necessary introductions.

"Margarita de las Fuentes, meet Alejandro Benevidez. He's from a village not far from here. Evidently it's too small to be recorded on any map," he added in answer to her unspoken question.

Transferring the Beretta to her left hand, she held out her right. "You can't imagine how happy I am to meet you, Señor Benevidez."

The gangly scarecrow hastily swiped a hand down his pants leg. His horny calluses rubbed rough against her palm. "Please, you must call me Alejandro."

"He's invited us to take shelter with him and his wife," Carlos told her.

"You'd best follow me quickly," the newcomer advised, "or night will catch us in the jungle and they will pull in the chair."

Pull in the chair? Margarita looked to Carlos for an interpretation. He lifted his shoulders and fell in behind their guide.

Abandoning the path Carlos had cut earlier, Alejandro squelched through the rain forest along some trail only he could discern. Before they'd traveled more than a few yards, a cloudburst swooped in, bringing an early dusk. After an initial pelting rain, a fine drizzle dogged them the rest of the way. Water dripped from Margarita's lashes and ran down her pants legs into her boots.

Rain and the onrushing night blinded her when at last they stumbled out of the forest and stopped beside a narrow gorge. The sounds of a rushing river rose from the darkness below.

"*Diablo,*" their guide muttered. "They've taken in the chair."

Margarita's curiosity got the better of her. "What chair?" she demanded, shoving back her wet hair.

Alejandro jabbed a finger upward. "The one that carries us across the river."

Squinting through the dark drizzle, she made out what looked like a stout, twisted rope outlined against the black sky. She followed its near end to a mahogany tree standing back from the edge of the gorge. The other end was lost in the murky darkness.

"Conceptión!"

The mooselike bellow had her jumping half out of her boots. Her ears were still ringing when a dog howled on the other side of the river. Another hound chimed in with the first. While the hounds set up a chorus of raucous calls, the listeners swatted mosquitoes and waited patiently. Finally, a woman shouted from the other side.

"Alejandro? Is that you?"

"*Si*. Send the chair."

Something scraped against the base of the mahogany tree. A rope, Margarita saw. A guide rope, she guessed, as Alejandro began playing it out hand over hand. Some moments later, a bumpy rattle announced the arrival of the mysterious chair.

At her first glimpse of the contraption, she widened her eyes. It wasn't much more than a small wooden crossbar dangling from some kind of a pulley. She was still trying to figure out how it worked when Alejandro graciously offered her first dibs.

"You hook your legs over the crossbar. It is very simple."

Too simple for Margarita's taste. Dubiously, she tested the wobbly support bar. "Are you sure this thing will hold me?"

"But of course. It takes me back and forth daily."

Since the rail-thin Alejandro probably weighed a good twenty pounds less than she did, that didn't particularly reassure her. Peering over the edge of the gorge, she eyed the river some fifty or so feet below. Oh, well. A spill into those dark waters couldn't get her any wetter than she already was.

Carlos stood beside her. Worry roughened his voice when he asked her if she could swim.

"Like a fish," she answered with only slight exaggeration. She preferred not to demonstrate her ability in the dark of night, however, weighted down with a vine backpack. In a river that might or might not be inhabited by bloodsucking leeches and other even less friendly life forms.

"I would go first, but...." He gave the twisted hemp cable a strong tug. "But it's better that I guard our rear until I know you're safely across."

"Right."

With the mental equivalent of crossed fingers, Margarita passed him the Beretta and tried to swing a leg over the crossbar. The primitive trolley dangled too high above the ground for her to climb aboard. Firm hands closed around her waist.

"Enjoy the ride, *querida*." Effortlessly, Carlos lifted her onto the precarious seat. "I'll join you on the other side."

"I certainly hope so," she muttered, wrapping her arms around the upright.

"Are you ready?" their guide inquired.

"I'm rea— Mother of God!"

Like a roller coaster with the brakes released, the crude wooden trolley shot straight down the sagging cable. Margarita squeezed her eyes shut, sure she was in for a dunking. The chair reached the bottom of the arc, climbed up a little, rolled back. Finally, it swayed to a halt with her boot heels dragging water.

"Hang on," Alejandro called cheerfully from above. "Conceptión will pull you up."

The guide rope creaked. The wooden pulley groaned. In fits and starts, Margarita was jerked upward to the other side of the gorge and greeted by Alejandro's wife. As short and round as her husband was tall and thin, she nodded politely as if strange females appeared in this remote corner of the jungle every night.

"Buenas noches, Señora."

"Buenas noches."

Taking time for only sketchy introductions, Margarita helped Conceptión ferry the men across the gorge. Once they had all gained the same side, Conceptión picked up her skirts and led the way up a cleared slope. A pack of dogs escorted the small group, barking furiously. Goats baaed and skittered away, their neck bells clinking. What looked like either a very skinny cow or an oversize jungle cat stared at them from the shadows.

Even on cleared land, the ground was so soggy Margarita sank to her ankles with every step. She caught the sound of small streams trickling down the slope toward the gorge and wasn't surprised to find that the people of the village had built their houses on stilts.

The half dozen or so dilapidated structures
squatted like drunken storks atop their pilings. Despite the darkness, Margarita could see that the
wooden walls sagged with rot and the cloth-
covered windows tilted at odd angles. Uneven
steps constructed of rough-hewn boards led to
doors covered only with oiled cloth. Drizzle ran
down corrugated tin roofs to splat on the soggy
ground below.

But the people who poked out their heads to see
what the commotion was about didn't appear con-
cerned that their homes looked ready to fall down
around their heads at any moment. At the sight of
strangers in their midst, the village's entire population poured out of their houses. Children, dogs,
chickens and a pink and white speckled shoat accompanied the handful of adults who gathered
around the newcomers.

Alejandro fielded questions while Conceptión
escorted her guests up a set of steps and ushered
them inside with the gracious hospitality of the
Madrileñan people.

"Our house is your house."

Ducking her head, Margarita entered the one-
room residence, lit only by flickering candles. Carlos followed, as did the rest of the villagers, dogs
and chickens included. Even the piglet joined the
gathering.

"Sit, sit," Alejandro invited with a wave of his hand. "First, you eat. Then you will tell us the news."

Praying that the sagging floor didn't give out beneath the crowd's collective weight, Margarita joined Carlos on a bench drawn up to the rough-hewn table. The others crowded around as Conceptión dished up bowls of rice and black beans, stacks of cold tortillas and tin mugs brimming with hot, sweet coffee.

The villagers waited politely until the strangers had wolfed down their food before resuming their eager questions. With no electricity to power radios, they obviously depended on the occasional visitor for news of the world.

The very occasional visitor.

As Carlos quickly determined, none of the inhabitants of this isolated corner of the rain forest had spoken to another outsider for upwards of a month or more.

"But I did see smoke from a cook fire earlier today," Alejandro commented. "Not far from where I ran into you. Someone follows you, I think."

"Someone does," Carlos admitted, his eyes grave. "But we don't know if that someone is my lieutenant and the rest of my squad, or a dangerous fugitive and his men."

"They are bad men, the ones with this fugitive?"

"Drug runners. From across the border."

Alejandro spit a brownish stream through the gap left by his missing front teeth. The spittle hit the piglet on the snout and sent it squealing.

"They are bastards," he muttered. "Scum who come in and cut into our meager profits."

The others murmured their agreement. Neither Carlos nor Margarita saw fit to comment on the fact that their host obviously dabbled in the illicit drug trade himself. So many of Madrileño's desperately poor farmers did, viewing it as a means to feed their hungry children. They didn't consider it their problem if rich, idle *norte americanos* chose to stuff the by-product of the coca plant up their noses.

For just that reason, Carlos had concentrated his crackdown efforts on the middle- and upper-echelon traffickers, those running major processing facilities hidden deep in the jungle and far-flung distribution networks. He wasn't after the little fish so much as the sharks and barracudas who fed on human weakness and misery.

"Tomás and I will go back across the river tomorrow to see who comes after you," Alejandro announced, hooking his arm around the shoulders of a skinny, grinning boy of seven or eight. "He's like a monkey, my grandson. He climbs the highest trees and no one sees him.''

''Will you also send your fastest runner to a village that has a radio?'' Carlos asked. ''If it's the criminal who follows, I want to call in reinforcements. These men are well armed,'' he added when his host puffed up his chest and appeared ready to argue his family's ability to take down a few Colombians single-handedly. ''With machine guns and perhaps shoulder-held mortars.''

A low murmur greeted that news. The men looked belligerent, the women worried. They'd had trouble here before, Margarita guessed. Bad trouble, judging by Conceptión's brisk manner as she pushed back her bench and shooed everyone away from the table.

''Our guests are wet and tired. You, Eliado, bring Carlos one of your shirts and dry pants. He would burst the seams of Alejandro's.''

A hulking young man hurried to do her bidding.

''And as for you, Señorita…'' Tapping a pudgy finger against her cheek, she eyed Margarita from the top of her dripping head to her muddy boots. ''For you, I think, my wedding dress.''

''I thank you,'' Margarita said from her heart, humbled that the woman would offer her most treasured possession. ''But, truly, it would be too fine for me.''

And too short. She topped the rotund Concepción by a good six inches.

"No, no, you shall have it. I was saving it for my granddaughter, but that one..." Her mouth pursed in disgust.

"Annuncia ran off with a gringo who came through last year," Alejandro announced. "A clumsy man who fell all over his feet, dropped his spectacles in the mud and collected ants in glass bottles."

"Ants!" Shaking her head over such foolishness, Concepción moved across the slanting floor to a row of woven baskets and dug through several in search of her wedding dress. The pungent scent of cedar bark drifting across the room assured Margarita that the baskets' contents hadn't succumbed to wet and mildew.

A smile played at Concepción's mouth when she returned with a white cotton blouse yellowed by age and a full, flounced skirt embroidered in an exquisite rainbow of colors. Fondly, she fingered the skirt's intricate pattern of vines, flowers and parrots.

"I began sewing this the very day I decided to let Alejandro court me. I knew long before he did that I would marry him." Her gaze lingered on Carlos for a moment before she caught Margarita's eye. "How long will you let this one court you before you marry him?"

Carlos hooked an eyebrow, obviously as interested in her answer to that loaded question as their hostess. For the life of her, Margarita couldn't come up with one. She floundered for a moment or two before Conceptión took pity on her.

"Ah, well, the marriage ceremony really matters little. After I bedded with Alejandro, three years passed before a priest could come to the village to bless our union. He baptized our son and first daughter at the same time." Her plump shoulders lifted in a shrug. "Once a woman takes her man to her bed, the rest follows as it will."

The recipient of that sage bit of philosophy flatly refused to look at Carlos.

"I found a nightdress for you," the older woman said, passing Margarita the pile of soft, cottony garments. "And some dry underwear. There is bark to scrub your teeth beside the bed, and soap if you wish it. Leave that jug on the table, Alejandro."

Her husband's face fell. "But, Ceptión, this is one of my finest batches."

"Our guests can sample it on their own if they wish. Come, it is late. We will go to our son's house so Carlos and Margarita may rest after their journey."

Abandoning the clay jug with a look of profound regret, the farmer followed his bustling wife through the oilcloth door covering. The dogs scurried after him, although the clutch of chickens and the piglet declined to go out into the drizzle.

A small silence descended, broken only by the patter of rain on the tin roof and the piglet's snuffling explorations under the table. Margarita clutched the cedar-scented garments to her chest and stared at the man watching her across the candles flickering on the table.

She could only imagine what she must look like after her dive into the moss and nose-to-nose encounter with the orange frog. Her hair straggled down her back. Carlos's fatigue shirt hung in heavy folds to her thighs. Mud oozed over her boot tops onto the floor.

He didn't present any more civilized appearance. His hair stood in wet spikes where he'd thrust a hand through it. Dark bristles shadowed his cheeks and chin. The black T-shirt was torn at one shoulder, stretched taut over the other shoulder. Beneath the short sleeves, his muscles gleamed wet and sleek in the candlelight.

Margarita's stomach clenched. Was it only a few hours ago she'd all but ripped that ragged T-shirt off his back? Only hours since she'd lost herself in those powerful arms?

Once a woman takes a man to her bed, the rest follows as it will.

Conceptión's words thundered in her head. As did Carlos's fierce promise.

The next time we make love, it will be in a bed.

We'll take it slow. So slow and sweet, you'll want to die of it.

Heat flooded her veins. Heat and something close to panic. She'd imagined she'd have days to sort through what happened this afternoon in the jungle, not mere hours. Time to find some middle ground between the aching, elemental needs Carlos stirred in her and her determination to remain her own person.

At this moment, with his eyes so intent on her, she could hardly remember her name, much less the person she thought she was. Dammit, she hated this confusion. Hated the flash of heat in her veins that got in the way of her thinking.

"You're wet to the bone," he said slowly, breaking into her chaotic thoughts. "You'd better change."

The borrowed clothes still tight against her chest, she looked around the single room. The closest thing to privacy was the shadowy niche beyond the mosquito-net-draped bed. She retreated behind the net and quickly stripped off. Despite the muggy heat, goose bumps prickled her skin as she removed her boots and socks, then peeled off her sodden jeans and shirt. She swore she could feel Carlos's eyes on her as she twisted her arms behind her back to unhook the red bra.

She heard a muttered curse, then the chink of clay against tin. Apparently Carlos had decided to indulge in some of Alejandro's home brew.

Swiftly, she tossed the bra aside, scrubbed the mud from her body with a rough cloth dunked in a bucket of water and pulled on Conceptión's nightdress. The cotton settled over her in cloud-soft folds and covered her from neck to mid calf. She wiggled out of her wet panties and stepped into the drawers her hostess had given her. They were the old-fashioned kind, high at the waist with legs that reached halfway down her thighs, but so comfortable Margarita sighed in pure, unadulterated bliss.

She was reaching for the scrap of fragrant bark to scrub her teeth when a thud of footsteps outside the door led to an exchange of male voices, followed by the sounds of Carlos, too, shedding his wet clothes. The broad-shouldered Eliado must have raided his possessions as ordered.

By the time she finished dragging a wooden comb through her hair, her entire body sang with the joy of being clean and dry. Wringing out her wet garments, she looked around for a place to hang them. Carlos, she saw, already had draped his fatigue pants and T-shirt on pegs pounded into the wall. Emerging from the shadowy niche, she arranged her clothes beside his.

That homey task done, she turned to find him comfortably settled on the bench drawn up to the table, a tin mug in his hand. The yeasty scent of fermented bananas drifted across the room.

This was another Carlos, she thought in quiet amazement. Another edition of the man she'd never seen before. The simple white cotton shirt of a farmer draped his broad shoulders. He'd exchanged his fatigue pants for well-washed cotton trousers and shed his boots. Madrileño's Deputy Minister of Defense appeared as much at home in these rough surroundings as he had at the Presidential Palace.

Evidently she, too, had metamorphosed. A smile played at the corners of his mouth as he skimmed a glance from her still-wet head to her bare toes.

"You look very different in that nightgown, *querida.* Like a little girl, with your face scrubbed clean and your hair hanging down your back."

At least until she moved into the light cast by the candles. Carlos caught the outline of her slender body beneath the gown and almost crushed the tin mug in his fist.

Holy Mother! And he'd thought those damned scraps of red silk and lace would drive him mad! They didn't begin to compare with the erotic play of thin cotton over dusky nipples. Or the shadowy suggestion of what looked like long drawers beneath the gown.

They were the sort his grandmother used to wear, for God's sake! Yet the idea of lifting that gown and sliding those old-fashioned knickers down Margarita's lean flanks sent a jolt of heat straight to his belly.

In the few seconds it took to toss down the rest of Alejandro's fiery brew, Carlos waged a fierce war with his rational self...and lost.

The mug hit the table. Shoving the bench back, he pushed to his feet. "Conceptión was right. It's late. Are you ready for bed?"

Her eyes widened. She flicked a glance beyond him to the net draped over the wooden platform in the corner. Her gaze swung back to Carlos. For long moments, she stared at him.

He sensed she was fighting her own internal battle, and knew the instant she surrendered. He saw it in the lift of her breasts beneath the thin cotton. Heard it in the long, slow sigh she breathed out.

"I'm ready."

Triumph stabbing through him, he swept her into his arms.

Chapter 9

Margarita awoke the next morning to a rare occurrence in the center of the rain forest—sunshine. Glorious, glittering rays. They flooded through the mosquito net draped over Alejandro and Concepción's bed to pool on the scratchy, handwoven sheets.

Basking like a cat in the golden wash, Margarita lay amid the tangled sheets and listened to the sounds of goat bells tinkling and a rooster crowing his heart out under the house next door. A languid contentment weighted her limbs. Smiling, she lifted her arms in a lazy stretch. An unexpected pull of sore muscles tipped her smile into a grimace.

Madre de Dois! She'd thought three days in the jungle would have loosened every ligament and tendon in her body. Apparently she'd exercised a few she didn't know she had last night.

Or rather, Carlos had.

She turned her head, frowning at the pillow beside hers. The scratchy ticking still bore the indentation from where he'd buried his head in it. He'd rolled out of bed before dawn with a whispered instruction to doze a while yet. Margarita had been only too happy to take him up on the offer. She needed sleep and time to regroup before she faced him in the light of day. Particularly after the incredible night they'd just spent.

Carlos hadn't exaggerated when he'd warned her that they'd take it slow. He was, she'd discovered last night, a master at slow. And tender. And erotic. He'd loved her in ways she'd never imagined, let alone thought to experience. Even now the insides of her thighs chafed from the scrape of his beard.

Her stomach clenched at the memory of how he'd cupped her bottom, lifted her hips and driven her to near madness. Never, ever had she guessed the magic a man could work with his tongue and teeth and wicked, wandering thumbs. Over and over, he'd brought her right to the brink of a shattering climax. Each time, she'd had to bite her lip to keep from screaming out her need. But nothing could hold back her sobs or her pleasure when, finally, he took them both over the edge.

Then, this morning, after what seemed like only moments of exhausted slumber, he'd ignored her sleepy protests and rolled her onto her stomach. Parting her legs, he'd canted her hips to his satisfaction and slid into her still slick depths once again. She'd come awake with the first slow drive. Within moments, she was writhing frantically and urging him to lunge harder, faster.

Carlos, damn him, had refused to hurry his pleasure. Vaguely, Margarita recalled beating her fists against the straw mattress and screeching like a cat with its tail caught in the door when the pleasure took her at last. She could only pray her cries hadn't awakened the whole village.

That hope died a mortified death when Concepción backed through the oilcloth a short time later carrying a small clay jug in one hand and a heaping plate in the other. She looked surprised to find her guest still in bed.

"Forgive me. I didn't mean to intrude upon you. I heard you, er, come awake with the roosters and thought you might want breakfast."

Margarita's face burned as she patted the sheets in search of her missing nightgown.

"It's under the bed," Concepción said with a

chuckle as she padded across the uneven floor to place her burdens on the table.

Spurred by the tantalizing aroma of hot chocolate, Margarita forgot her embarrassment and dropped the cloud of soft cotton over her head. Feet bare, she joined her hostess at the table. Her taste buds danced with joy when she saw the contents of the high-piled plate.

Mounds of golden fried banana were topped with sour cream made from goat's milk, she guessed. Or perhaps from the milk of the skinny cow she'd glimpsed last night. The inevitable black beans that formed the staple of every Madrileñan meal swam in a pool of thick broth. Her mouth watering, Margarita scooped them up with tortillas still warm from the outdoor oven.

"This is wonderful," she said between hungry bites.

Concepción accepted the compliment with a smile. "Our cows have no meat on their bones, but they give plenty of milk. If only we could get the milk to market before it sours…"

Shrugging off the impossible task of hauling milk through miles of uncharted jungle, she poured a mixture of clear water and the juice of tart, sour oranges into a mug. Margarita gulped it down, drinking in energy with the tangy liquid.

"I'm making a pig of myself," she said as she

rolled another tortilla and dug it into the beans. "I'll have just one more and save the rest for Carlos."

"He ate earlier with the men, before he left."

"Left?" The tortilla halted a few inches from her mouth. "Left for where?"

"He and Alejandro and our little Tomás went back across the river, to see if they can spot those who follow you."

The beans and bananas congealed in a heavy lump in Margarita's stomach. Carlos had gone to hunt down their pursuers, taking only Alejandro and his young grandson…and leaving her safe and snug with the women.

She tossed down the half-eaten tortilla. Anger rifled through her, swift and fierce. He'd taken off without a word to her. Without asking her opinion in the matter or even considering that she might have one.

Damn him! After all they'd been through, all the ground they'd covered together in the past few days, surely she'd earned the right to be consulted.

"They'll be all right," Conceptión said in a reassuring voice, mistaking the reason for her sudden rigidity. "Alejandro knows this corner of the jungle like the back of his hand. He won't let your man walk into a trap."

"Carlos is not my man," Margarita answered

tightly. "He's his own man. Very much his own man, apparently."

The older woman's glance darted to the rumpled bed. Her brows rose skeptically, but inbred courtesy kept her from contradicting her guest.

"I will leave you to dress. The rest of the women are just outside, plucking chickens. Come and join us when you will. We'll have a feast tonight in honor of your visit, yes?"

She left Margarita still simmering with anger at Carlos—and now riddled with guilt. These people were so wretchedly poor. She hated for Conceptión to sacrifice her precious chickens but knew better than to wound her pride by protesting.

Although raised to appreciate the comforts that wealth afforded, she was also too much her mother's daughter to sit idle when there was work that needed doing. Maria de las Fuentes had scrubbed floors, boiled laundry in a big black caldron and hoed the kitchen garden on a large ranchero before she won the eye and the heart of the neighboring landowner's son. Proud of the fact that she'd come from the land, she made sure her own brood appreciated the people who tilled and toiled on it.

Quickly, Margarita finished her breakfast and retreated to the nook beside the bed to strip down and scrub away the lingering aftereffects of the

night's activities. Her mouth tightened as she
dragged a rough, wet cloth over her body. Carlos's
scent seemed to have invaded her pores.

She had just stepped into Conceptión's old-
fashioned drawers when she felt a tiny tremor
against her breast. Instantly, her palm went to the
gold locket. The vibration was so small, so
slight…and so frustrating! Even after three days,
SPEAR hadn't given up trying to contact her. If
only she had some way to return the signal!

The locket tingled against her breast for a minute or two. Stopped. Began again. Stopped. Thinking it might be some kind of code, Margarita flattened her fingers over the piece and held her
breath. The signal didn't come again. Sighing, she
finished dressing.

The loaned wedding skirt and blouse were far
too fine for the task of plucking and scalding chickens, however. For that, Margarita pulled on her still
damp jeans and Carlos's fatigue shirt. Once
dressed, she smoothed the handwoven blankets
over the straw mattress, then went outside to join
the other women.

Bubbling laughter, bright sunshine and abject
poverty greeted her. Pausing on the porch while
her pupils adjusted to the dazzling light, Margarita
surveyed the scene. Most outsiders would have
been dismayed by the muddy track that constituted

the village's only street, not to mention the houses that looked about to tumble off their stilts at any moment. Beyond the tip-tilted, tin-roofed structures, sloping fields dotted with charred tree stumps stood guard against the jungle that would reclaim the entire village in less than a month if allowed.

Yet none of the women clustered on benches placed in a haphazard circle appeared the least daunted by their surroundings. Feathers flew as their hands kept as busy as their tongues. It only took Margarita a moment to realize they were offering candid advice to a young woman whose husband had apparently become so aroused by the sight of her nursing her babe that he'd attempted to lift her skirts while the child was still at her breast.

"Rogerio tried the same thing when I nursed my first," a heavyset woman related with a snort. "I ground the seeds of nasturtium into his beer. For three days, he could barely make it to the fields to release himself. After that," she finished smugly, "he left me alone until I was ready for him."

"Which was probably the very next week," the woman next to her jibed. "Not that I blame you. He's a bull, that Rogerio. As is this so-handsome Carlos, judging from the groans that came from

Conceptión's house this— What? Why do you poke me?''

She followed her companion's nod and spotted Margarita on the porch. Chagrin took the laughter from her lively face for a moment. But only a moment. With the earthy candor of people who live their lives close to the cycles of the earth, she grinned.

''I meant no disrespect.'' Nudging the woman beside her with one hip, she made room for the newcomer on the bench. ''But tell us, this Carlos of yours, is he as much a man as he looks?''

Surrendering to the inevitable, Margarita laughed and joined the women's circle. ''More.''

Hot, sweaty and thoroughly disgruntled, Carlos swatted at a particularly persistent mosquito and waited his turn on the wooden trolley. Alejandro had gone first. Little Tomás was halfway across the gorge, clinging to the upright support like the monkey his grandfather had named him.

The boy's sharp eyes and climbing skills had yielded nothing this morning, though. They'd backtracked a good way into the jungle, stopping often for Tomás to shinny up the vines and gain enough height to search above the canopy for the telltale signs of human passage. No birds flapped into the sky. No warning screeches echoed above the treetops. No smoke curled into the sky.

The only sign they found that indicated persons other than Alejandro had followed Carlos and Margarita's trail was a small fire pit with the charred remains of several candy wrappers. Someone, evidently, had a fondness for chocolate-covered coconut.

Who?

One of the escaped prisoner's men? One of Carlos's?

The uncertainty ate at Carlos. That and the fact that whoever had followed them had been closing in when Alejandro crossed their path. The timely decision to detour to a village so tiny it didn't show on any maps had thrown their pursuers off their trail. For now.

Having come this far, whoever tracked them wouldn't give up. It was only a matter of time until they, too, doubled back and found their way to the river gorge.

Instinct told Carlos that it was the escaped prisoner who risked the dangers of the jungle to hunt someone he perceived as an even greater danger to himself. Instinct and the questions Margarita refused to answer about her involvement with the man.

Her stubborn recalcitrance rubbed Carlos raw.

She knew more about this criminal than she would admit. Knew more about a lot of things than she'd ever admitted. Carlos would bet his last *centavo* she hadn't learned how to take off a rat's head with a single shot from her father.

He'd been tempted to shake the truth out of her a time or two. For a moment last night, he'd even considered holding back, using the passion that had her writhing and crying out in need to get at the truth.

To his profound disgust, he hadn't been able to bring himself to resort to sexual blackmail. She had only to open those incredible violet eyes, cry his name in a voice hoarse with desire, and everything but the need to pleasure her pushed to the back of his mind.

And this morning…

This morning he'd been too caught in the grip of his savage hunger to focus on anything but the satiny lines of her back and the rounded hips slamming against his thighs. Just the memory of their wild half hour before the dawn tightened Carlos's throat.

Like a fool, he'd assumed that once he and Margarita finally tumbled into bed, they'd satisfy the desire that had simmered between them for so long and move to the next higher plane. He knew better now. He'd be walking with a cane before he got enough of the stubborn, sensual woman who looked as beautiful in mud as she did in flame-colored silk.

Or chicken feathers.

When Carlos reached the other side of the gorge and trudged up the slope beside Alejandro and Tomás, he almost tripped over his own feet. None of the images of Margarita he'd locked away in his mind in the past months included anything close to this flushed, laughing woman with feathers stuck in her hair and a headless chicken gripped tight in one fist.

Unaware of his arrival, she chattered with the woman next to her, all the while ripping feathers from the hapless fowl with a skill that amazed Carlos. *Dios!* Was there nothing this woman couldn't or wouldn't do?

The fact that he was so slow to discover her many and varied secrets intrigued and irritated Carlos all over again. Consequently, he wore something close to a scowl when he and his companions reached the women. Nor did his mood improve when Margarita lifted her head and caught sight of him. Her laughter died, and a distinct chill frosted her eyes. Passing her half-plucked chicken to the woman next to her, she rose and dusted her hands on the seat of her jeans.

"Did you find anything?"

"A fire pit and a candy wrapper," he answered curtly, knowing what she'd ask next and frustrated by his inability to answer it.

"Could you tell who made the fire?"

"No."

She digested that in silence for a moment. When she spoke again, the chill had seeped from her eyes to her voice.

"Don't you think you should have told me that you intended to go into the jungle with Alejandro?"

"You were asleep." Not particularly happy about the way she took him to task in front of the others, he hooked a thumb in his belt. "I woke you earlier—"

A plump, dark-eyed matron snickered.

"—but you went back to sleep. The trek through the jungle must have tired you out," he added blandly for the benefit of the others.

That resulted in an outright snort. "*Something* tired her out."

Wondering just what the devil these women had been discussing in his absence, Carlos took Margarita's arm. "Why don't we talk about this while I sluice off some of this mud and sweat? Alejandro said there's a pool just a little way from here."

For reasons totally beyond his comprehension, that raised a storm of laughter among the women.

Even Margarita's lips twitched. Carlos looked at
Alejandro, who shook his head.

"What was that all about?" he asked Margarita
as she fell in beside him.

"Nothing."

He cocked an ear to the smothered laughter behind them. "It doesn't sound like nothing."

"It was no big deal. Really." To his surprise,
her cheeks pinked. "Just a reference to a silly accident that happened the last time Elena and her
husband bathed together at the pool."

Avoiding his eyes, Margarita ducked into Conceptión's house to grab a bar of soap and their
clean clothes. Carlos couldn't know, of course, that
the little accident at the pool left the twenty-two-
year-old Elena pregnant with her sixth child. Or
that the young mother's hilarious account of the
challenges of satisfying her man's sudden urge to
couple underwater and at the same time keep them
both from drowning had convulsed her audience.

Unfortunately, it had also brought home to Margarita the fact that she, too, was an accident waiting to happen. Neither she nor Carlos had exercised any kind of restraint. Nor had they used any
protection. The last thing they needed to worry
about right now was the complication of a possible
pregnancy.

Lost in his thoughts, Carlos kept silent as they

crossed a muddy field dotted with tree stumps to the pool formed by two streams just a dozen or so yards before they plunged over the gorge. He kept his distance in the cool, green pool, showing not the least inclination to attempt the same underwater feat as Elena's husband. Margarita floated under an awning of cascading ferns and fragrant orchids while he attended to the serious business of scrubbing down.

He made short work of it. A quick, masculine soaping of hair, arms, chest, belly. A swift immersion. A shake of his head to get the water from his eyes. When he scraped a palm along his chin, frowning, Margarita guessed the bristly growth must itch like the devil in this heat.

"I'll get rid of this beard while you finish," he said after another scrape, confirming her guess. "Then we need to talk."

"About?"

"About what we do next."

Lathering his cheeks and chin, he tossed her the soap and waded to the pool's edge. Margarita treated herself to the sight of his long, sleek flanks and tight buns before turning away to soap her heavy mass of hair.

By the time she'd dried off and draped herself in Conceptión's blouse and colorful embroidered skirt, Carlos had managed to scrape most of the soap off his cheeks and was working on his chin. With a long-bladed knife and no mirror to aid him, he'd also managed to nick himself in several places. Tiny rivulets of red ran down his neck, faded to pink, then disappeared in the dark hair of his chest.

He grunted, and another spot of red blossomed on his cheek.

"Here, let me."

Folding her knees, Margarita sank down beside him and took the evil-looking knife. It was smaller than the machete, but just as sharp.

"Have you ever shaved a man before?" he asked cautiously.

"Often."

His brows snapped together. "Who?"

"My father," she drawled. "Before he found an electric razor that cut close enough for his satisfaction, he used to like my mother to shave him. When she was busy, I filled in. Hold still."

She found a certain satisfaction in performing this small service for Carlos. His departure this morning without a word still rankled, but her annoyance receded into the background as she fell into a familiar rhythm. Dipping her hand in the pool, she wet the drying soap, then slid her fingers along the line of his jaw to draw his skin taut. The knife blade followed smoothly in her wake. A flick of her wrist, another stretch, another smooth scrape.

She leaned forward, twisting a little to get at the soap on the underside of his chin. The movement dragged down the drawstring neckline of her blouse and flattened her breast against his bare, muscled shoulder.

A queer little quiver began in her chest where his shoulder pressed so intimately. Her soapy fingers slowed their stroke, loving the feel of smooth tendons and supple skin. Loving the sight of Carlos's face tipped to the sun, eyes closed, his black lashes fanned against his cheeks.

Absorbed in her task and the rugged symmetry of his face, she almost missed his sudden stiffening. But she couldn't miss the way the dark eyes so close to hers flew open, then narrowed to slits. He jerked his head away from the blade, startling her. His gaze locked on the front of her borrowed blouse.

"What is that?"

Confused by the sudden fury in his voice, she shook her head. "What's what?"

His jaw tight, he wrapped a fist around the small pendant that had slipped outside her drawstring neckline. Holding her tethered by the seemingly delicate gold chain, he lifted his hand. The flat disk lay on his palm.

''This.''

Her stomach sinking, Margarita identified the source of that funny little quiver in her chest a few moments ago. The damned locket had begun vibrating again.

Chapter 10

Carlos's fist closed around the pendant. Tethered like a goat at the end of a rope, Margarita needed only one glimpse of the fury in his eyes to know she'd just run out of maneuvering room.

"Tell me," he snarled. "The truth this time, dammit."

Still she hesitated. She'd lived her secret life for so long, reported only to her contact at SPEAR all these years. Yet the shadowy head of their agency had always stressed that he'd recruited his agents for their ability to think on their feet as much as for their loyalty and discretion. There was only one absolutely unbreakable rule in SPEAR. If agents ever find themselves with their backs to the wall, they should toss *all* rules out the window.

Margarita's back was definitely to a wall, this one in the shape of a very angry, very dangerous deputy defense minister. His black eyes lethal, Carlos used the locket to drag her even closer. The chain cut into the skin at the back of her neck. She could almost feel the heat of his fury leap from his skin to hers.

"Tell me!"

"I work for a top-secret agency called SPEAR."

He cursed. The single, viciously descriptive noun left no doubt in her mind what he thought of the secret organization.

"I have for almost three years now."

His nostrils flared. Anger vibrated deep in his chest as he slowly, so slowly, unclenched his fist. "And this?"

"It's a signaling device, to let me know when headquarters wants me to contact them."

Disbelief slashed across his face. "All this time? You've been in contact with this SPEAR all this time?"

"No! The locket only receives signals, it doesn't send them."

He didn't believe her. She saw the doubt darken his eyes, replaced an instant later by flat distrust. As though she was one of the enemy. Someone whose every word had to be measured against the facts. Racked with guilt and hating herself for it, Margarita wrenched the gold pendant out of his hand.

''The thing's been vibrating off and on all morning. I thought at first it was some kind of coded message, but I'm damned if I can figure it out.''

He didn't respond. His gaze was shuttered. Without moving so much as a muscle, he'd withdrawn from her. Intellectually. Emotionally. Physically.

Dismay pulled at Margarita. She knew in that instant she'd destroyed more than his trust by withholding the truth. She'd shattered as well the intense bond they'd forged these past few days.

''I couldn't tell you, Carlos. Not while there was a chance I could still maintain my cover.''

''Of course not,'' he said with a cool dispassion that cut through her like a machete. ''Someone who plays the kind of games you do can't afford to trust anyone.''

Anger piled on top of her guilt and put a snap in her spine. ''I've told you before, what I'm doing isn't a game.''

Her flash of heat strained the iron hold he'd slapped on his emotions. For a moment, she thought he'd lash out at her again, prayed that he would. Anything would be better than this cold, deliberate withdrawal.

"All right. You've told me what it isn't. Why don't you tell me exactly what it is."

Pulling in a long breath, Margarita fed him the bare facts. How she was recruited while finishing her master's at Penn State. How she'd received the same training as the other agents but specialized in intelligence gathering instead of field operations, with a particular focus on the Latin American drug trade. How her position at the Ministry of Economics had dovetailed perfectly with the work she did for SPEAR.

His mouth curved in a sardonic twist. "And I, fool that I was, believed it was my kisses that set you trembling in my arms. I see now it was just delight at the information you were extracting with every breathless sigh."

"Oh, for—" With some effort, she bit down on her too-ready temper. "I never tried to draw information from you, Carlos. Just the opposite, in fact. Where do you think that tip came from? The one that led to the big bust last week?"

"That was you?"

"Yes."

Torn between guilt and a determined pride in the work she did for SPEAR, Margarita waited for him to process that bit of information. He didn't speak for several moments. When he did, he sounded sharp and hard, like a man who'd decided to make the best of a situation he didn't like but had to deal with.

"Start at the beginning. I want every detail. Who is this man who has been trying to kill you? How did he end up in Madrileño? Why did the captain of the guard think he knew you? What's SPEAR's interest in him?"

The questions came at her like bullets from an Uzi. Raking back her hair, Margarita supplied the scanty details as she knew them.

"We started picking up vibes about seven months ago that someone had declared a sort of personal vendetta against SPEAR. Only recently did we even have a name to attach to the rumors."

"And that is?"

"Simon. No one knows his background or where he came from, only that he's got connections to a host of illegal and underground groups, ranging from white supremacists to Middle Eastern terrorists."

"Not to mention Latin American drug lords." Carlos glared at her, his jaw tightening. "And SPEAR sent you to interrogate this thug? I hope I don't meet the man who issued that insane order any time in the near future."

Her eyes flashed a warning. "I can hold my own

against the Simons of the world...as I think I've proven these past few days.''

"You proved a number of things," he agreed with a biting undertone. "Not the least of which is the blind stupidity of a man who thought he was in love."

Thought he was in love? The implication hit Margarita like the backhanded slap Simon had delivered in the cave.

"Carlos..."

"Finish what you have to say."

"There isn't much else," she replied stiffly. "I couldn't get anything out of Simon about his background or motivation. Only that he wears his scars like a flag and intends for Jonah to see them soon.

"Who's Jonah?"

Silently cursing her slip, Margarita was forced to peel back another layer of the onion. "He heads SPEAR. I know even less about him than Simon, but I trust him with my life."

"At least there is someone you trust," Carlos said in a carefully neutral tone that cut even worse than his anger. Pushing to his feet, he scooped up his shirt and dragged it on.

Margarita rose, as well, fumbling for an answer. There wasn't one.

"Is there anything else you want to tell me?" he asked coldly.

Yes! That she was sorry she'd had to mislead him for so long. That these days in the jungle had ripped away so many layers of doubt...and added so many of confusion. That she couldn't imagine spending her days...or nights...with anyone but him. Pride and the stubborn knowledge that she'd only done what Carlos himself would do in the same circumstances kept her silent.

"We'd better get back to the village so you can get changed and gather your things."

He slapped on his belt, hooked the buckle and turned away. Frowning, Margarita fell in beside him.

"Are we leaving?"

"You are. Alejandro's son-in-law is going to take you downriver in his dugout. There's some white water south of here, but nothing Eliado can't handle."

"You've got it all scoped out, have you?"

"That's right."

"Just what will you to be doing while Eliado and I shoot the rapids?"

"Alejandro and I are going back and pick up the trail at the pit fire we found this morning. I'm not leaving the jungle until I find out what happened to my men."

She dug in her heels. He kept going for another few paces, then turned with an expression that warned her he was in no mood for an argument from anyone, least of all from her.

Tough! As lacerated as she was by the knowledge that she'd lost Carlos's trust, she refused to abrogate either her responsibilities or her mission to hunt Simon down.

"I'm going with you and Alejandro."

"The matter's not open to negotiation."

"I'm not negotiating. I'm telling you flatly that I'm going with you."

"The hell you are."

"You brought your men into the jungle to rescue me. Whatever happened to them is as much my concern as yours. Besides," she added nastily, "you need me. We both know which of us is the better shot."

He strolled to her, menace in every line of his taut body. "You know, there was a moment this morning when I seriously considered tying you to the bed and getting the truth out of you any way I could. Now that I know, the idea holds even more attraction."

"Why don't you hang onto that thought until we get back to San Rico?" she asked, putting everything she had into the sultry suggestion. "Sounds like fun to me."

His jaw dropped. A look of comical astonishment slackened his features and broke the tension clawing at Margarita's chest.

"Why are you so surprised? I've entertained a few fantasies about you, too. As the women of the village so correctly surmised, you're much a man, Carlos. Very much a man."

She brushed past him, giddy with relief and satisfaction at having gotten in the last word. She had a long way to go before she regained his confidence and trust. She knew that. But the heat that leaped into his eyes gave her a huge shot of hope that she might just pull it off. All she'd need was a little persistence, a little ingenuity…and a few hours alone with Carlos under a mosquito net.

She wouldn't get them tonight, she thought ruefully. Not with Alejandro accompanying them on the search for Carlos's men. But afterward. When this was over. Back in San Rico, at her apartment. Or his office.

On his desk.

Under it.

Anywhere she could get him alone.

Shaking her head, she forced the erotic images to the back of her mind. She needed to focus, to prepare herself mentally for the trek into the jungle.

As it turned out, she and Carlos never made it into the jungle. They almost didn't make it back to the village.

They had just stepped out of the dense growth ringing the pool into the muddy field when a burst of gunfire blazed from the far side of the gorge. Bullets splatted into the earth. Muck spouted like miniature geysers all around them.

''Get down!''

Enforcing his shouted command with a shove, Carlos sent her sprawling toward a nearby tree stump. Margarita landed facedown in the mud for the second time in less than twenty-four hours. He dropped almost on top of her.

The air whooshed out of her lungs. With his weight pinning her down, she couldn't draw in so much as a gasp. Thankfully, he rolled off her a moment later and wrestled the Beretta out of its holster.

The automatic cracked right beside her ear, temporarily silencing the shooter on the far side of the gorge. Over the ringing in her ears, Margarita heard someone scream a vile oath, answering shouts, the screech of monkeys and parrots taking flight. Cordite stung her nostrils, burned her eyes.

For a minute, two, she sprawled beside Carlos, straining to sort through the sounds, trying to see through the undergrowth on the other side of the gorge. She caught a rustle of ferns, saw a strangler vine sway. Her heart stopped. The shooters were heading south along the rim of the gorge. Toward the crude little trolley!

The realization hit Margarita at the same instant it did Carlos. Cursing, he speared a glance down the gorge. The hemp cable strung across the river sagged lazily in the sun.

Margarita didn't have to tell him what someone like Simon would do to Alejandro and his family if they got in his way. She saw the brutal awareness in the look he turned on her.

"We've got to cut the ropes."

"Give me the gun." She rolled into a crouch behind the stump. "I'll provide protective fire."

He hesitated for only a second. They were equals now. On the same team. For the moment, anyway. He handed over the automatic without a word, then dug in his vest for the spare clips.

"Stay as low as you can," she instructed tersely. "Use the tree stumps for cover."

To her utter astonishment, his lips twitched. "Yes, ma'am."

That tiny half-smile exploded the last of Margarita's doubts. At that moment, on her knees in the mud, with the jungle behind them and a murderous band of drug runners ahead, she knew with absolute certainty that she loved this man. What in the world she'd do about it was another matter, however.

And now certainly wasn't the time to tell him about her little epiphany. Carlos needed every ounce of concentration he could muster for his sprint across the field.

"Ready?"

He nodded, his thigh muscles bunching. Margarita two-fisted the Beretta, propped her wrists on the tree stump and reminded herself that the automatic had drawn up and to the right just a hair when she'd taken down the javelina.

"Go!"

Zigzagging wildly, Carlos made it halfway across the field before bullets ripped though the air again. It took everything she had to keep her sights on the red flashes and not on Carlos. Her heart hammering, she squeezed off a single shot.

An agonized scream tore across the gorge. The machine gun skipped, stuttered, was silenced. Knowing she had only moments, perhaps seconds, until one of the other men snatched the weapon and resumed fire, Margarita took off after Carlos.

She caught up with him on the run. Or thought she did. Only after they'd gained the shelter of the village did she realize he'd danced a jig in the field, deliberately exposing himself to draw the hostile fire until he could shield her body with his.

Before she could protest such idiocy, Alejandro came running toward them, his gray mustachios flying. His gnarled hands clutched the oldest, rustiest shotgun Margarita had ever seen. Behind him raced his sons, sons-in-law and grandsons, all armed with machetes.

"Is it the drug runners?" Alejandro panted.

"Yes."

"*Dios!* Those pigs will regret the day they fired on our village."

Carlos stilled their bravado with a dash of cold reality. "They're armed with at least one semiautomatic. We can count on rifles and handguns, as well."

"Do we know how many come?"

His dark eyes whipped to Margarita. "One less than started out this morning, thanks to the sharpshooter among us."

The men treated her to a round of admiring glances.

"We have to take down the cable before they cross the river," Carlos told them. "I'm sorry."

Alejandro waived an airy hand. "It is of no matter. We will weave another to replace it, just as we do each time it falls."

"Each time it *falls?*" Margarita gaped at him. "Last night you said it took you back and forth across the river daily."

"And so it does. When it doesn't fall."

"Well, this time we'll aid its fall," Carlos said decisively. "Margarita and Alejandro will cover me while I hack it down. The rest of you, take your women and children into the jungle."

Just in case.

He didn't say it, but the unspoken understanding passed among the men. They knew as well as Carlos that the chances of one Beretta and an ancient shotgun holding off a band of drug dealers armed with the latest weapons were slim to almost non-existent.

Gulping, Margarita swept a glance down the dirt track that constituted the village's only street. The tree anchoring the cable stood alone at the bottom of a sloping field. Carlos would have no shield, no protection except the tree itself and the meager cover Margarita and Alejandro could provide.

"Maybe we should *all* go into the jungle," she heard herself say. "Escape and evasion is always a viable option when—"

She stopped abruptly, her lips tightening as the locket quivered against her breast again. Stilled. Quivered again. For pity's sake! Did SPEAR think she had nothing better to do than sit around and try to interpret these signals?

"We let no one drive us from our homes, poor

as they are,'' Alejandro said fiercely. ''I will stand beside you and fight.''

Carlos drew out his machete, the steel singing on leather. ''With luck, it won't come to that. Get the women and children out of the village. Quickly. Time runs against us.''

In fact, Margarita saw several anxious moments later, time had run out.

She crouched behind one of the pilings that supported the house nearest the cable, her heart in her throat as she watched Carlos take a swing at the woven hemp stretched across the gorge. Bean-stalk thin Alejandro sheltered behind another piling.

The machete's first whack still reverberated on the heavy air when at least a dozen armed men emerged from the undergrowth across the gorge, guns blazing. Carlos twisted violently and plastered a shoulder to the stout tree trunk. With the murderous fire slicing the air around him, he couldn't move, much less swing the machete. Grimacing in desperate concentration, he angled the blade over his head and sawed awkwardly at the cable.

The Beretta barking, Margarita returned the vicious fire. She thought she caught a glimpse of a hideously scarred face, but lost it almost immediately as the men on the other side of the gorge

dived for cover. Safely hidden, they resumed their
barrage.

Alejandro's ancient shotgun roared. The sound
of the shot ka-boomed like a cannon through the
empty space under the house, almost deafening
Margarita. He emptied the second barrel right after
the first, then ejected the spent shells and reloaded.

Her ears buzzing, sweat stinging her eyes, Margarita carefully spaced her fire. She only had two
spare clips. If Carlos didn't cut the cable... If they
had to retreat and fight a rearguard action...

Focusing on the task at hand, she blanked her
mind to everything but Carlos pinned to the tree
trunk. The hemp cable. The rain of fire from the
other side. So fiercely intent was she that Alejandro
had to shout frantically to get her attention.

"Margarita! Listen! Listen!"

She shook her head in a vain attempt to clear
the ringing in her ears. "What?"

"Helicopters!"

Only then did she catch the distant whap-whap-
whap of rotors slicing the air. Carlos picked up the
sound at almost the same instant. He froze, the
machete raised above his head.

With the house above her, Margarita had no
view of the sky, no way to tell from the chopper's
markings whether it carried government troops or

reinforcements Simon had called in. Desperately, she shouted to Carlos.

"Can you see them?"

"I... Yes!"

She had time for a single prayer. Please, *please* let them be ours.

Then the treetops began to rattle, the whining roar of engines filled the air, and all hell broke loose.

Chapter 11

The chopper came down fast on the level ground near the top of the slope, the 50 mm machine gun mounted in its waist blazing. A second chopper swooped in a second later. Commandos in jungle battle dress poured out of both and added to the murderous fire.

The dense growth lining the other side of the gorge disintegrated. Branches flew into the air. House-size ferns toppled. Even the stout mahogany tree anchoring the cable splintered.

The woven hemp cable hung together by a few shreds for a second or two before it, too, came apart. The handmade trolley slid down a severed length and sailed majestically into the gorge.

Not now, Margarita wanted to shout. Not when the men on the other side were beating a frantic retreat. Those who could still move, anyway. Ducking, dodging, some slithering on their bellies, they aimed a few desperate shots over their shoulders before the jungle swallowed them up.

"Hold your fire!"

Swiping the mud and sweat from her eyes with her arm, Margarita squinted at the commandos. Their leader had already charged past her, heading for Carlos. All she saw was the man's back.

Margarita emerged from behind her piling, intending to join the two men, only to freeze as she caught a flutter of white on the far side of the gorge. One of the fleeing men popped out of the underbrush. Took aim. She needed only a single glimpse to know it was that bastard Simon...and to see instantly who he had in his sights!

"Carlos!"

The scream ripped from her throat at the same moment the commando lunged through the air. He and Carlos went down in the mud. Shots burst out. Simon dropped from sight. The gunfire stuttered into silence.

"Get a chopper revved up," someone shouted behind her. "We need to get to the other side of the gorge. They're escaping."

Margarita paid no attention to the burst of activity behind her. Terror clawing at her chest, she plunged down the muddy slope. Before she could reach the two figures sprawled on the ground, they had untangled themselves and pushed to their feet.

Relief pumped into her in waves, made her clumsy. She tripped over her own boots and ended up on her knees. The two men started toward her. Concern etched sharp grooves in Carlos's cheeks.

"Are you all right?"

"Yes, I..."

Her jaw went slack. Eyes widening, she stumbled to her feet and gaped at the commando in black face paint and jungle fatigues.

"Marcus!"

"In the flesh, babe."

Grinning, the SPEAR agent stepped around Carlos and planted a hard, muddy kiss on her mouth.

"That," he announced, "is for scaring the hell out of me by disappearing the way you did. I have other messages for you, which I'll deliver once we round up the rest of your friends."

Half laughing, half flustered and wholly delighted by his timely arrival, Margarita introduced him to the man who'd gone still beside them. Very still.

"Marcus, this is Carlos. Carlos Caballero."

"I guessed as much," Marcus said, shoving out

his hand. "I've heard a lot about you in the past few days, *commandante*."

"Have you?" Carlos drawled. "Oddly enough, I've heard nothing of you."

"Margarita and I are old friends," he said, as if that was enough to explain his sudden appearance in the jungles of Madrileño.

Carlos lifted a brow at that, but before the SPEAR agent could launch into the cover story Margarita knew he'd have ready, a dark patch on his sleeve snagged her gaze.

"Marcus! Is that blood on your sleeve?"

"Probably," he replied with cheerful unconcern, glancing at the stain. "That last shot grazed me."

Carlos's brows snapped together. "You took a hit?"

"Guess I caught a corner of the bullet that was aimed at you, my friend."

Judging from the amount of blood that had soaked his sleeve, it was far more than a graze. Margarita was about to point that out when the sudden sound of an engine powering up spun them all around.

The men were scrambling aboard one of the choppers. A short, stocky figure detached himself from rest and plowed down the slope, greeting Carlos with a wide grin.

"It's good to see you, *commandante*."

Returning his grin, Carlos clapped a hand on his aide's shoulder. "It's good to see you, too, Miguel. How many of our squad are with you?"

"All of them."

"Good man! You got them out."

"With a little help," the lieutenant admitted, pitching his voice to a shout to be heard over the increasingly high-pitched whine. "Half the bastards kept us pinned down while the other half went after you. We were almost out of ammunition when Señor Waters here arrived with reinforcements."

His glance enigmatic, Carlos nodded to Marcus. "It appears I'm doubly in your debt."

"Consider all debts paid in full once we find the man who took Margarita hostage."

"I'll find him," he promised tersely. "I have a score to settle with the man." He ran a quick eye down the bloodied sleeve. "Miguel and I will mount the hunt. You'd better take care of that arm. Even a graze can turn deadly in the jungle."

There wasn't time for more. The helicopter's blades had begun to slice the air, moving faster with each rotation. Carlos said something to Margarita, but the whirling rotors chewed up the words and spit them out. With another nod to Marcus, he turned and started up the slope.

"Wait!" Her hair flying madly around her face,

Margarita dashed after him. "I'm coming with you."

"Your friend is in more pain that he admits. Get him seen to and take charge of the operation here. I'll go after the ones who've escaped into the jungle."

"But..."

"I'll see you in San Rico."

For the second time in as many minutes, Margarita found herself in a man's arms. Carlos's kiss was just as swift as the one Marcus had given her, but far more thorough. He left her standing in the mud, her hair lashing her cheeks.

The chopper lifted off as soon as he and Miguel climbed aboard. Once airborne, it banked sharply and roared across the gorge. Margarita watched it skim the treetops like a giant dragonfly buzzing after its prey. All too soon, it disappeared behind the towering curtain of green.

Sighing, she turned to Marcus. His blue eyes followed Carlos's chopper for a moment before switching to Margarita. His mouth creased in the same teasing grin that had gotten them both through their tortuous survival training, when they'd shared everything from dew scraped drop by drop from leaves to the threadbare blanket they'd stolen from an unsuspecting enemy.

"Well, well. Looks like I've got some competition to worry about."

She brushed aside his joking attempt to make more of their friendship than there was.

"The only thing you need to worry about right now is that bullet hole in your arm. If you recall, the last time we practiced field first aid on each other, you threatened to quit SPEAR altogether if they let me anywhere close to a needle again."

His wince was only half feigned. "I remember."

Cradling his injured arm, he started up the slope. Margarita took one look at the white grooves bracketing his mouth and slipped her arm around his waist. With his good arm draped across her shoulders, she steered him toward the second chopper.

"How did you find us?"

"Your signal receiver."

The locket. The little oval piece that now lay innocuously inside the torn, muddied drawstring blouse. She should have guessed that its furious buzzing earlier had special significance. Sure enough, Marcus confirmed that the techno-wizards at SPEAR had been working night and day since her disappearance.

"It took them two days to figure out how to magnify the signals enough that they could be picked up with high-powered scanners. Another

two days for us to position the scanners in Madrileño. I'm surprised the thing didn't burn a hole in
your skin when it started pulsing."

"It came close a time or two." She hesitated,
then added, "Carlos felt it vibrating this morning."

If Marcus wondered just how Carlos had gotten
close enough to notice the movement of the locket,
he didn't say so. "So he knows you work for
SPEAR?"

"I had to tell him."

"No one's going to argue with that. From the
information we've gathered about the man in the
past few days, it's obvious he's one of the good
guys."

"Yes." She threw a glance over her shoulder at
the distant treetops. "He is."

"Anyone else know?"

She dragged her attention back to find Marcus
regarding her with keen blue eyes. "What?"

"Anyone else know that you work for
SPEAR?"

"Not that I'm aware of."

"I'd better brief you on my cover, then."

"Which is?"

With his good arm, he swept off the crushable
jungle hat that covered his thatch of blond hair and
attempted a sort of a bow. "Marcus Waters, bounty
hunter, at your service, ma'am. I've been tracking

Simon for months for a wealthy client whose daughter almost ODed on the drugs supplied by his network.''

Margarita had to admit it was perfect. A soldier of fortune, a modern-day gunslinger who demanded high dollars to bring in fugitives.

''I managed to get close enough to one of his men to plant a bug, which is what let me muscle in on the rescue operation and what everyone thinks led us to you. Got it?''

''Got it.''

''Okay, babe, let's go to work.''

Moments later, the second chopper was in the air. The pilot positioned it in a hover on the far side of the gorge and lowered a heavily armed squad. Margarita went with them, searching among the wounded for Simon without success. She could only hope Carlos and Miguel would track the bastard down.

They hoisted the wounded into the chopper and brought them to the village. The medic who'd accompanied the strike force went to work stabilizing his patients for transport, Marcus included.

''You're lucky,'' the young medic commented. ''The bullet took off a chunk of muscle, but missed the bone.''

"Yeah," Marcus replied, wincing at the sting of disinfectant, "real lucky."

Leaving him in capable hands, Margarita went to say goodbye to Alejandro and Concepción and the others. The muddied skirt and torn blouse drew an abject apology from her.

"I'm so sorry about your wedding finery."

"No matter. It served its purpose." A smile tugged at her generous mouth. "For you as well as me, I would guess from that kiss Carlos left you with."

Maybe. Everything had happened so fast, so many emotions had crowded on top of each other. Margarita hadn't forgotten Carlos's fury when she'd told him about Simon and her work with SPEAR. Or that moment in the field, when her blinders fell away and she knew without a doubt that she loved him. They'd sort things out when they got to San Rico. She hoped.

With a smile for Concepción, she promised to send her another dress. "Or better yet, you and Alejandro must come for a visit, and you can pick out just the one you want. I'll send another chopper for you."

She was only too happy to fly in a commercial charter for these people. As poor as they were, they'd sheltered her and Carlos with unstinting generosity. Remembering her plunging roller-coaster ride across the gorge, she made a mental note to be sure the chopper brought in steel cable and planking for a footbridge.

"I'll also speak to my uncle about cutting a road through to the village," she promised Alejandro. "So you can get your milk and cream to market before it sours."

A flurry of excited comment greeted that. In the midst of the chatter, Alejandro asked curiously, "Who is your uncle?"

"The President. Of Madrileño," she added at his blank look.

His jaw sagged under the drooping gray mustachios. "Mother of God! You told me your name, but I didn't... I never... There are so many de las Fuentes," he finished helplessly.

"I know. It's a very common name. One of our ancestors must have been particularly prolific."

The whine of engines revving up hurried the rest of her goodbyes.

Within minutes, she and Marcus and the team transporting the prisoners were airborne. While Marcus conducted an in-air interrogation of the more coherent among Simon's men, Margarita borrowed a headset and eavesdropped on the radio exchanges between the pilot and the crew of Carlos's chopper. Her heart jumped when the pilot radioed that they'd sighted what looked like a possible trail and were lowering a pursuit team via the jungle penetrator. Carlos went with them to coordinate the effort from the ground, instructing the chopper to continue the aerial search.

The search was still in progress an hour later, when the first helicopter touched down at San Rico airport. The pilot had radioed ahead that he was bringing in wounded as well as Señorita de las Fuentes, so Margarita wasn't surprised by the string of ambulances and limos lined up along the runway.

Relinquishing her headset with reluctance, she waited until the more seriously wounded had been loaded onto stretchers, then climbed out with Marcus. Her feet had barely touched the tarmac when a small avalanche of relatives surrounded her. After a joyous and somewhat tearful reunion with her mother, father, brothers and assorted sisters-in-law, she dodged the inevitable demand to know why in the world she'd gone to the prison and offered herself as a hostage in exchange for the guard.

"Papa, please. Let me get Marcus to the hospital first. I'll answer all your questions later."

"Marcus?"

As one, her relatives turned to the injured agent, taking in his smeared face paint and bloodied sleeve. Her father in particular gave him a keen once-over.

"You're the American bounty hunter. The one who planted the bug."

Marcus stepped into his role without so much as a blink. "Yes, sir."

Maria de las Fuentes brushed past her husband to offer the injured man her heartfelt thanks. Still slender and vibrant after thirty-eight years of marriage and five children, she pressed a kiss on Marcus's cheek.

"You must come and stay with us while you recover from your wound."

"Well, I..."

Margarita interceded. "We've already decided he's going to stay at my place until he's fit to rejoin the hunt. That way, I can tell him everything I learned about the man he's looking for."

It was nothing less than the truth. Debriefing Marcus about the hours she'd spent with Simon constituted her first priority.

A delicate frown creased her mother's forehead. Pointedly, she searched the group of men mingling around the chopper.

"Where's Carlos?"

"In the jungle."

Eight hours later, Carlos still hadn't returned and Marcus had transformed Margarita's condo into a combination command post and recovery center.

The SPEAR agent had rigged a communications link directly to the military net monitoring the search for Simon. Every radio transmission from the chopper pilots crackled over the speakers hooked to a specially configured laptop computer.

While they waited for the results of the search, Margarita gave Marcus a thorough debrief. What details she couldn't remember, he pulled out of her. Disdaining the painkillers the docs had given him, he carefully matched the information she provided to what he'd extracted from the prisoners during the flight to San Rico. When Jonah made contact with them on a high-tech, untraceable phone line, Margarita fed the results to SPEAR's chief.

Jonah was quietly exultant over the destruction of Simon's drug network in Latin America. Between them, Marcus and Margarita had identified all but a few of his key suppliers. Once the suppliers were shut down, he'd lose his primary source of income for his worldwide clandestine operations.

Jonah also found the fact that Simon seemed to take a sort of perverse pride in his disfigurement extremely interesting. "I'll get the docs to factor that into the psychological profile they've constructed so far. It might shed some light on what's motivating him."

Recalling the evil that had flared in the man's one good eye, Margarita silently wished the shrinks luck.

"He didn't give you any insight into what he has planned next?" Jonah asked.

"No. But he was clear on one point. He intends for you to see him. Soon."

"I'll be ready," the chief said softly.

She didn't doubt it. Whoever or whatever he'd been in his former life, the man she knew only as Jonah had assumed an awesome mantle of responsibility when he'd shed his former identity to take over SPEAR. Over the years he'd recruited a highly skilled cadre of agents, put them through training that would give lesser mortals instant cardiac arrest, given them the autonomy to make instant life-and-death decisions in the field. Every one of them knew he'd shaped them and the agency based on his experiences and could only guess how brutal those must have been.

"You did well, Margarita. Very well."

The praise went a long way to mitigating her lingering self-disgust over the way she'd ended up at the wrong end of Simon's gun.

"What do you think the chances are that Caballero will find him?"

She hesitated, hating to admit the truth. "Not good. As I learned only too well in the past week, the jungle swallows you whole. There were times I didn't think we'd ever find our way out.''

And God knew Simon was a master at escape and evasion. He'd eluded SPEAR for months.

"If anyone can find him, Carlos can," she said, absolute certainty mixed with a quiet pride.

Jonah signed off a moment later. She found Marcus watching her with an unreadable expression on his face.

"If I was a betting man, I'd say you and Carlos got pretty close while you were dodging bullets and hacking your way through vines.''

"We did," she admitted slowly. "Very close. The jungle has a way of stripping things down to the basics.''

Keen blue eyes sharpened. "Do I hear a but in there?''

"No.''

"Try again, babe. This is Marcus you're talking to, remember? The guy who booted you in the butt to get you through the tangle of barbed wire in the first obstacle course we ran.'' A sun-bleached blond brow cocked. "Having doubts about our friend Carlos?''

Margarita didn't answer. What she felt for Carlos was her business. The problem was, she was damned if she could figure out what to do about the way she felt.

Catching the inside of her lower lip between her teeth, she looked past Marcus to the sliding glass doors that gave onto her tiny balcony. The spectacular view of a blazing red sun hanging low over a sea of molten gold filled her vision, but her mind saw only a dark, primeval rain forest. A bed of ferns. A bronzed warrior.

When Carlos emerged from the jungle, would he revert to the man she'd known before? The suave, calmly confident politician whose conservative views of marriage clashed in every way with hers? Could she still love him so desperately if he did?

She got the answer to at least one of those questions the very next night.

Chapter 12

Marcus was in Margarita's kitchen, pouring himself another cup of coffee, when he caught the sound of a small thud in the hall outside the front door.

He almost missed it. What passed for evening rush-hour traffic in Madrileño's capital drifted through the sliding glass doors, left open to the balmy January night. A newscaster pitched the latest headlines on the TV. The shower in Margarita's bedroom had just kicked on and drummed a steady beat against the tiles.

If he hadn't been on his fourth cup of coffee since dinner and so jagged after a frustrating twenty-four hours spent waiting for word from the field, Marcus might have shrugged the sound off.

The fact they hadn't received any report suggested Simon was still unaccounted for, and Marcus wasn't about to dismiss any noise, however slight, outside Margarita's door. He wouldn't put it past the bastard to slip back into San Rico and pick up where he'd left off in that cave.

His gut still tightened whenever he thought of Margarita's flat, unemotional account of her hours with Simon. Marcus had dragged out every detail, from the bonds that had made the bruises still visible on her wrists to the brutal backhanded slap and promise to make her beg long and hard before he gave her so much as a sip of water.

If—when—Marcus got his hands on him, he'd personally insure that scar-faced piece of slime did some serious begging himself.

With a fierce hope that it was, in fact, Simon who'd made that noise in the hall, he slid the carafe onto the coffeemaker and reached down to draw a lethal little snub-nosed Smith & Wesson from his boot.

The sound of another thump brought Marcus flat against the wall beside the front door. Trusting the instincts that had kept him alive during his years in the field, he decided to take advantage of the element of surprise. A single wrench threw the door back on its hinges. Before it hit the wall, Marcus had the .38 leveled on the figure in the hall.

Narrowed black eyes locked with blue. For several seconds, neither man moved.

"Christ, Caballero!" Cocking his wrist, Marcus tipped the barrel of the .38 upward and thumbed down the hammer. "Arriving unannounced like that is a sure way to get yourself killed."

The face stubbled with two days' growth might have been cut from granite. "I wasn't aware I had to announce myself to you, Waters."

He speared a glance into Margarita's airy living room, then brought his hooded gaze to Marcus.

"Playing watchdog?"

No fool, the agent sensed the quicksand underlying the soft question. One false step, and the bog would suck him in. Well, he'd never been one to tiptoe around anything.

"Yes. Until we heard from you, I wasn't letting Margarita out of my sight."

Approval took some of the fierceness from the hawklike stare. "I was counting on that."

Hefting his gear, Carlos strode into the airy living room. A single glance at the high-powered rifle and bulky backpack slung over his shoulders told Marcus the source of the thumps he'd heard. He followed, slamming the door behind him.

"Simon?" he asked urgently.

Carlos shook his head.

"Dammit!"

The ice came into the black eyes. "You're not any happier about it than I am."

"Sorry. I didn't mean that as a slam against you personally. SPEAR's been trying to collar that son of a bitch for several months now. Even with all the resources at our disposal, we haven't been able to nail him. We don't know where or how he learned his survival tactics, but he sure as hell learned them well."

Carlos thawed enough to unsling his rifle and prop it beside Margarita's colorful jungle-print sofa. The heavy pack followed.

"I thought we had him late yesterday afternoon," he said in a voice laced with frustration. "We followed his trail down a steep gorge. Night dropped while we were still only halfway down. The damned path was so narrow, we had to inch the rest of the way with our back to the walls."

Not a fun exercise, Marcus imagined, even with night-vision goggles.

"By the time we reached the bottom, the tracks disappeared. My guess is he took to the river and floated downstream during the night. We conducted an air search for forty miles along the river, but the canopy was so dense it was difficult enough to maintain radio contact while zigzagging through the trees, much less spot anyone moving beneath.''

''So that's why we didn't hear from you. Margarita said the jungle could swallow someone up whole.''

''Speaking of Margarita...''

He angled his head, cocking a brow at the sound of the shower drumming against the tiles of the bath. When he brought his gaze to Marcus, the agent felt the sand shift under his feet again. In the blink of an eye, they'd moved from the professional to the personal, and neither man pretended otherwise. Still, he wasn't prepared for what came next.

''How long have you been in love with her?''

After his initial surprise, Marcus felt a wry grin tug at his mouth. So much for his debonair, light-hearted approach. Margarita still didn't have a clue that he'd fallen for her, and hard. Caballero, apparently, had picked up on it immediately.

He didn't see any point denying the obvious. ''I think I lost it the first time she narrowed those gorgeous violet eyes and crunched down on the rice beetle I insisted she had to eat. We went through survival training together,'' he added by way of explaining his menu choice.

Carlos nodded. ''I guessed as much. Otherwise she would have told me about you.''

The idea that Margarita shared everything with him except her association with SPEAR stung. In all the time Marcus had worked with her, she certainly hadn't told him anything about the Deputy Minister of Defense. Curiosity had him countering swiftly.

"How long have you wanted her?"

"A lot longer than she's wanted me," Carlos replied with a shrug.

Marcus had just congratulated himself on still being in the running when his rival shattered his hopes of ever making it to the finish line.

"My ego had taken quite a beating…until the past few days."

Marcus most definitely didn't need to hear that. Yet he didn't blind himself to the truth. There was a reason he buried his feelings for Margarita in the playful banter they tossed back and forth. She didn't see him as anything but a friend. She never had.

He was damned if he'd admit as much to this hard-edged Madrileñan, though.

Nor did he feel the least compelled to hint that Margarita was having second thoughts about whatever happened between her and Caballero in the jungle. This cowboy would discover that for himself soon enough. Folding his arms, he waited for the next round in what was turning into a definite skirmish. It wasn't long in coming.

Making himself at home, Caballero strolled into the kitchen and helped himself to coffee. He downed a healthy chug, then regarded Marcus steadily over the curling steam.

"I haven't forgotten that I owe you."

"You don't owe me anything."

"You got to my men just in time. You took the bullet meant for me. I owe you." He took another long swallow before issuing a friendly but unmistakable warning. "Just don't make the mistake of thinking my debt to you in any way involves the woman in that shower."

Unaware of the minor testosterone war being waged in her living room, Margarita squeezed her eyes shut and lifted her face to the lukewarm water.

The headache lurking at the base of her skull still throbbed. Nor had she been able to soak away her tension. Even after draining the hot water tank and pickling herself to a prune, she couldn't seem to loosen the blasted knot between her shoulder blades.

Sighing, she slouched against the tiles. She hadn't grabbed much more than an hour or two of sleep since she and Marcus returned to civilization. The grueling debrief had eaten up yesterday after-

noon. They'd spent most of the last night and all
of today pacing, waiting for the communications
link to intercept and spit out radio transmissions,
hoping for news of Carlos. The last transmission
had come just before midnight, when he and Miguel and his men were inching their way to the
bottom of a gorge.

Oh, God! What if Simon picked them off one
by one while they were strung out on the narrow
path? What if he'd laid an ambush for them at the
bottom? The panic she'd held at bay all day twisted
her stomach. She should have insisted on going
with Carlos. She should have...

The glass shower door clicked open.

Margarita's lids flew up.

Water sprayed into her eyes. Not enough to
blind her, just blur the face of the man who joined
her in the stall. She didn't need to see his features
for her heart to take a sudden, joyous leap. She'd
recognize those muscled shoulders and broad chest
blindfolded. Before he'd wedged himself fully into
the stall, she threw herself forward.

"Carlos!"

His shoulders hit the glass shower door and
bounced it open. Heedless of the water that rico-
cheted off their bodies and onto the Berber carpet,
Margarita smothered him in kisses. When she finally came up for air, water beaded her lashes and

his beard had scraped a raw patch on her chin. She disregarded both to ask the question he so obviously expected.

"You didn't find him?"

"No. We lost him at the bottom of a river gorge. I'm sorry."

She disguised her biting disappointment by raking back the black hair plastered to his forehead. Short and curling just a little with the wet, it slid through her fingers like cream.

"You don't have to apologize for anything," she said fiercely. "Simon's been leading SPEAR on a wild-goose chase for months."

"So Waters reminded me."

"Waters." Her hand stilled. "Oh. Right. Marcus."

She'd forgotten the agent in the other room. Fumbling for a way to explain his presence in her condo that didn't sound as though she *had* to explain anything, she chose her words carefully.

"The docs wanted to keep him in the hospital for a night or two, but we needed a secure place to debrief, so we, ah, decided he'd stay here."

"Good thinking."

She blinked away the beaded water, surprised at his complacence. She might even have commented on it if his hands hadn't slipped down to cup her wet buttocks at that precise moment. Contorting his tall frame, he nuzzled the neck just under her left ear.

"Since you've finished your debrief," he murmured against her skin, "we reopened discussions and decided he'd be more comfortable at my place."

"What?"

She tried to pull back. Carlos wasn't having any of it. His fingers curved under her rear, anchoring her.

"I gave him my keys."

"But…"

"He's already packed up his gear and left."

She was still digesting that abrupt turn of events when Carlos flexed his arms. In a smooth play of muscle and tendon, he drew her up, inch by tantalizing inch, until she hooked her arms around his neck and her legs around his lean flanks.

By the time her mouth reached his again, Margarita had forgotten Marcus, forgotten her headache, forgotten everything but Carlos. Her breasts flattened against his chest. Eager fingers raked through his hair, held his head at just the right angle for her kiss.

Her slippery eagerness almost unseated her. Bending a knee, he cradled her bottom on his thigh. The movement freed one of his hands to slide over her hip, curve up her waist. Tender rough with calluses, it made its way to her nape and tipped her head back.

"I missed you."

She smiled through the pulsing water. "I missed you, too."

He hesitated, as though he wanted to say more, but Margarita wiggled to find a comfortable spot on his thigh, and his jaw clamped shut. Instantly, his body hardened under her.

Delighted with the reaction, she wiggled again. The skin stretched tight across his cheekbones.

"Margarita…"

Her attention divided between his ragged breathing and the rigid shaft that had sprung to life just under her bottom, she tipped her head.

"We didn't use any protection in the jungle," he growled.

"I know." Her eyes held his. "It worried me."

"It worried me, too. I don't want anything from you you're not ready to give."

Her heart flip-flopped in her chest. She ached to tell him she was ready to give him anything and everything he asked, but his mouth tipped in a wicked grin, and the words got caught in her throat.

"I'm better prepared this time…if I can let you go long enough to get to my pants."

"I'll tell you what," she murmured, squirming off his thigh. "We'll get to them later. What I have in mind right now only requires you, me, that bar of soap and a little maneuvering room."

With a grin to match his, she reached for the pale yellow oval. The French-milled soap had been a Christmas gift from her cousin. Somehow, she suspected Anna wouldn't particularly appreciate the use Margarita intended to put her gift to.

The bar slid over Carlos's shoulders, leaving a foam of jasmine-scented bubbles in its wake. Slowly, Margarita worked her way down his chest, his ribs, his stomach. When her fingers encircled his jutting shaft, he drew in a sharp breath.

Her own breath ragged, she soaped the satiny skin and bone-hard muscle. All too soon, play wasn't enough. She wanted to touch, to taste, to take every inch of him inside her. Her back to the tiles, she slid slowly down, tracing a path with her mouth and tongue.

Legs spread, palms planted against the tiles, Carlos shielded her from the pelting water and fought to hang onto his control. With Margarita's hands and lips and tongue so busy and eager, it was only a matter of moments until he lost the fight.

With a sound halfway between a groan and a grunt, he snagged her arms to pull her up and lost his balance in the process. Or maybe she dragged him down. Carlos didn't know which and didn't care. They tumbled out of the shower in a tangle of wet legs, slick arms and hungry mouths.

Eventually, they made it to the bed.

The carpet would take days to dry, Margarita thought sleepily some hours later. Sated and drowsy and lost in the joy of clean sheets and the man beside her, she felt herself sinking into blissful oblivion. She was almost there when Carlos brushed a tangle of hair from her cheek.

"Rita."

"Mmm?"

"Last night, when we were inching our way along that damned gorge..."

She lifted one eyelid. Blinked at the broad expanse of bronzed skin covered with squiggly black chest hair. Tipped her head. As sleepy and boneless as she felt at that moment, her heart thumped. God above, what a sight to open her eyes to!

He loomed over her, head propped on one hand, face intent. Stubble darkened his cheeks. His hair glistened wet and glossy black. If she'd had so much as an ounce of energy left anywhere in her body, she would have lifted a hand to smooth the rumpled silk. All she could manage was a smile.

"What about last night?"

"All I could think about was taking Simon down so he could never hurt you again."

Margarita couldn't argue with that, although she would have preferred to do the down-taking herself.

"I'd give my life to keep you safe."

The simple declaration moved her profoundly. "Carlos, I…"

"Wait. Let me say this." A rueful smile lit his eyes. "I rehearsed this speech all the way back to San Rico."

Fully awake, she stared at him.

"I love you, Rita."

Her mouth opened. Closed. She gulped out a shaky reply. "I…I love you, too."

It wasn't quite the passionate response Carlos had hoped for, but it would do. For now.

"I want you in my life," he told her. "Any way I can have you. As my wife. My lover. My friend. You set the parameters, as long as they include me."

She shifted, angling her head to see him more clearly. He sensed what was coming before she framed the questions.

"What about my work with SPEAR? And the Senate seat my uncle wants you to run for? I don't know if I can give up everything I am to become the perfect little politician's wife."

"As I've already told you, I'm happy with the job I have at the Ministry of Defense. And as for your work with SPEAR..."

His gaze dropped to the locket resting between her breasts. He hated the damned thing, hated the thought that its silent signal could pull Margarita into danger at any second. Yet she'd proved herself more than capable of handling whatever situation she landed in.

"I saw a side of you this week that stunned me. And aroused me," he admitted wryly. "You're incredible, Margarita."

She was too intelligent not to recognize the dilemma that put him in. Understanding shimmered in her amethyst eyes. "You admire that part of me but can't quite get comfortable with it."

"I won't lie to you. My skin crawls whenever I think of you putting yourself in the line of fire. And I don't particularly like the idea that you and Waters might disappear together for weeks at a time."

"There's nothing between Marcus and me," she interjected quickly. "We're just friends."

Carlos opened his mouth, snapped it shut. He wasn't about to let the SPEAR agent get between him and Margarita. But neither would he rub salt in the other man's wounds by revealing his feelings for her.

Besides, Carlos had his own feelings to worry about right now, not the least of which was how the hell he was going to clamp down on his almost overwhelming need to shelter and protect the woman he loved from the Simons of the world.

"I can live with what you do for SPEAR. I don't like it, but I can live with it."

"Jonah kept me working a desk until this situation came up," she said slowly. "I had hoped for more field assignments, but…"

She was trying to find a way. Trying to reconcile her needs with his. Carlos recognized that even as he fought the urge to encourage her to stay firmly anchored to her desk.

"We'll work it out," he promised fiercely.

Chapter 13

"You and Carlos will work it out."

Sighing at her mother's confident prediction, Margarita poured herself another glass of iced coffee laced with sinfully rich cream, leaned back in her chair and tipped her face to the sunshine flooding her parents' flower-filled patio.

Maria de las Fuentes had been issuing variations on the same theme for the past week. As had Margarita's father, brothers, uncles, cousins and assorted friends. Everyone seemed to think the fact that Carlos had moved into Margarita's condo a week ago meant they should start shopping for wedding presents.

Everyone except Anna. Beautiful, sulky Anna glared at Margarita from across the table.

"You're going to ruin his chances for that Senate seat by living openly with him," her cousin said with a waspish snap. "This is Madrileño, not the States."

"Anna!"

The younger woman's mouth set stubbornly at her aunt's mild rebuke. "Margarita doesn't appreciate him. She never has. I'd make him a far better wife than she would."

"Too bad he doesn't want you," her cousin returned sweetly.

Anna's face heated. "I could make him want me."

"I don't suggest you try," Margarita drawled.

Her flush deepening, the younger woman shoved back her chair. "You can't have it both ways, cousin. Either you love him and want to join your life to his, or you don't."

That stung. Trust Anna to know just where to stick the barb in. Margarita said nothing as her cousin took leave of her aunt and flounced out.

"Don't let her bother you," Maria advised calmly. "This is a new century. Even in Madrileño, no one will hold the fact that you and Carlos are sleeping together against him if he decides to run for the Senate. Although it would look better if you two were married when the campaign kicks off, of course.''

"Of course."

Unperturbed by the sardonic reply, Maria shifted to another tack. "When does this bounty hunter of yours go back to the States?"

"He's not my bounty hunter."

The innocent lift of the mother's brows didn't fool the daughter for a second. Maria disapproved of the hours Margarita had spent in Marcus's company during the past week, helping with the manhunt still underway.

It was a massive effort. Marcus and Carlos had teamed together to coordinate the search. Margarita had taken leave from her job to help, as well. She'd been so busy, she'd hardly drawn a full breath for days. Unfortunately, most of the leads they'd followed had led nowhere.

She could blame no one but herself for that. Word had spread like jungle fever about the road and footbridge she'd promised the villagers who'd helped take down the drug runners. The state-run television studio had run a news story on it, along with the composite sketch of Simon drawn from details Margarita had provided. Now, every headman in Madrileño schemed to find a way to bring the same munificence to his village. Dozens of reports of the disfigured *norte americano* who'd accompanied the drug runners had surfaced in the past week. So far, none of the reports had produced results.

"Marcus will probably go back to the States soon," she said in answer to her mother's question. "Unless something turns up at this fishing village we're driving out to this afternoon."

That produced another lift of brows. "Carlos doesn't object to the hours you spend with this man?"

"No."

Far from objecting, Carlos had demonstrated a surprising forbearance. Margarita might have chalked it up to his vow not to interfere with her work for SPEAR if she hadn't begun to suspect the two men had formed a private alliance, one designed exclusively for her protection. They made sure she was never alone. During the day, she worked with Marcus in the command center he'd set up in Carlos's study or interpreted for him when they drove or choppered out to chase down rumors. Her nights...

Sweet heaven above, her nights! She didn't dare think about the wild hours in Carlos's arms with her mother sitting across the table.

She should have known Maria wouldn't miss the flush that heated her cheeks. "Carlos is a good man,'' she said quietly. ''One I would be proud to see in the Senate or as my daughter's husband.''

Margarita dodged the second issue to answer the first. ''I don't think he wants to run for the Senate. He says he's content at the Ministry of Defense.''

''Your uncle still hopes to convince him. He needs someone strong to carry that seat.''

''Someone with ties to our family, you mean.''

''That, too.''

Idly, the two women contemplated a humming-bird milking nectar from the hibiscus flowers that climbed over the patio wall. The tiny bird hovered at the mouth of a massive bloom, its wings beating iridescent green against the orangey red. Fascinated by the aerodynamics of its stationary midair position, Margarita reached for her iced coffee.

''You know,'' her mother mused, ''if Carlos doesn't run for the vacant seat, perhaps you should.''

The coffee went down the wrong pipe. Gasping, Margarita choked out a demand to know if Maria was serious.

''Completely. You're smart. Well educated. You come from a family dedicated to public service. What's more, you've proven your abilities at the Ministry of Economics.''

''But…''

''With Carlos as defense minister and you as a

senator, the two of you could shape Madrileño's future long after your father and uncle retire.''

She gaped at her mother. Her conservative, contented mother, who'd happily tended to every domestic detail for decades while her husband went about the serious business of men.

''Don't look so stunned, *niña*.'' Maria's face softened into the smile that had won Eduard's heart so many years ago and kept her children totally devoted to her. ''Do you think I expect my daughter to make the same choices I made? You must follow your heart wherever it leads you.''

Margarita still hadn't recovered from that astounding piece of advice when her mother dropped another minor bombshell.

''I hope, though, your heart would lead you to give the same service to your country you've given to this so-secret organization you've become involved with.''

''Wh— What organization?''

''I don't know the name of it and don't wish to,'' Maria said primly. ''Just think about what I've said.''

Margarita thought about it all during the drive to the fishing village fifteen miles south of San Rico. Not even the hairpin turns and sheer hundred-foot drops edging the winding mountain road distracted her.

They certainly distracted Marcus, however. Hunched over the wheel of Carlos's sleek little BMW, he muttered a curse at every switchback turn, interspersed with low whistles at the spectacular views.

"Would you look at that!"

Margarita dragged her thoughts from her astounding conversation with her mother. When she saw the scene that had captured his stunned gaze, a smile poked through the emotions punching at her from all sides.

Madrileño at its most beautiful lay below them. Jungle-covered mountains cascaded to the edge of the sparkling turquoise sea, fringed by a sugar-sand beach. Beside the row of boats dragged up on shore, fishing nets dried on poles. Their colorful glass buoys winked merrily in the afternoon sun. Tucked beneath the palm fronds was a jumble of thatch-roofed huts.

The idyllic tranquillity of the scene viewed from the high, winding road gradually dissolved into the wrenching reality of poverty. At a sharp bend, Marcus turned off the road and inched the BMW down a side spur that was little more than a sandy track mixed with shell. Any resemblance to a road disappeared completely a hundred or so yards from the village.

"Our last hurricane probably washed it away," Margarita guessed.

"Which could be why they decided to report this supposed contact with Simon. Maybe they figure to get a new road out of the deal from the softhearted President's niece."

"Maybe."

Knowing from experience she'd sink up to her ankles in the soft sand, Margarita unstrapped her sandals and tucked them in her straw tote. Her button-front sleeveless dress in a cool beige cotton flapped at her knees as she forged a path through the dunes.

Marcus trudged beside her, his boots churning up sand and shells. He'd appropriated a few dress shirts from Carlos along with the BMW, but today he'd opted for one he'd picked up at the outdoor market in San Rico. The Panama-style shirt hung loose and comfortable over khaki chinos. With wrap-around yellow-mirrored sunglasses and blond hair poking from under a ball cap worn back to front, he looked more like a grad school dropout on a cheap vacation than a secret agent on a mission.

"Whew!" He wrinkled his nose. "Guess they had a good day with the nets."

The stink of fish entrails baking in the sun was their first warning that the dwellings that had looked so picturesque from the road were considerably less charming up close. As she plowed through the sand, Margarita saw that the thatch roofs had grayed with age and no doubt housed huge populations of beetles and geckos. Rusted barrels on stilts provided reservoirs for drinking water. Dogs lazed in the sun, and hairy little pigs rooted in the trash under the houses.

At least electricity had reached the village. A single line straggled through the palms to one of the huts topped, incongruously, by a tilting TV antenna. The rousing beat of a Latin dance number pulsed through wooden shutters propped up with a stick to catch the breeze.

With their approach, a chorus of barks and howls joined the music and brought the villagers from their varied pursuits. A few fishermen weathered by sea and sun to a leathery brown dropped the nets they'd been mending and sauntered over. They were joined by a scattering of women and children too young or too old for the mandatory schooling Margarita's uncle had instituted even in these remote villages.

The inhabitants greeted Margarita and Marcus with the friendly gregariousness of most Madrileñans. When she introduced herself, excitement rippled through the small group.

"You're the niece of *el Presidente*," one of the fishermen exclaimed, aiming a quick glance at his companions. "The one who builds the footbridge."

"Yes, I am," she admitted, ignoring her fellow agent's I-told-you-so grin. "We were told you've seen the man we're looking for, an American with a scarred face and one good eye."

Half a dozen heads bobbed. A young woman with a baby on her hip answered for them all. "Yes, yes. He came down from the mountains late at night. Him and one other."

"When?"

"Two nights ago."

"They paid Ramon to take them in his boat," a grizzled fisherman volunteered.

"Take them where?"

"To another boat." He gestured vaguely toward the sea. "It was waiting for them."

Marcus met Margarita's eyes. They'd need something more specific than "another boat" to make the drive down to this isolated village worthwhile.

"Which of you is Ramon?" he asked, reserving judgment but clearly wanting to be convinced.

"My husband hasn't come in yet," the young

woman replied, hitching the baby higher on her hip. "He should be back soon. Paulo says the sea bass have stopped running."

Courteously, she offered them the shade of her house and orangeade or beer to quench their thirst.

Marcus accepted a beer for both of them and declined the invitation to wait inside. "Perhaps someone could show us where this man and his companion emerged from the jungle."

No one seemed to know the exact spot.

"It was late," one of the fishermen explained. "We didn't see them until the dogs started barking. But I think, perhaps…there."

Following the line of his outstretched arm, Marcus nodded. "Thanks. We'll check it out."

Margarita accompanied him along the wave-washed beach, warm beer in hand. "You don't really think we'll find anything to mark a trail after two days of tropical rainstorms, do you?"

"Nope."

"Then why are we going through this pointless exercise?"

She couldn't see his eyes behind the mirrored sunglasses, but his grin took on a wicked tilt.

"What if I tell you I just wanted to kill time by taking a stroll along a beautiful beach with an even more beautiful woman?"

"I'd say the sun has probably gotten to you."

''What? You think just because I've seen you with beetle juice dribbling down your chin, I can't get past that unsavory image to the delicate flower underneath?''

''Yeah, right.''

The delicate flower snorted and plowed ahead, only to be brought up short by the hand Marcus wrapped around her bare arm.

''What if I tell you I was thinking of more than a stroll along the beach?''

Sun-bleached blond brows waggled above the glasses in a lecherous leer, surprising a sputter of laughter from Margarita. ''I'd say the sun had *definitely* gotten to you.''

''You would, huh?''

The cocky smirk was all Marcus. So was the teasing banter. Yet Margarita caught just a hint of something different in his rich baritone, something she'd never heard before.

''How are things going with you and Caballero?''

The question came out of the blue, startling her. Was there something in the air today? First her mother. Now Marcus.

''They're going,'' she answered vaguely.

Marcus digested that in silence for a moment. ''Did he tell you what we talked about the first night he showed up at your apartment?''

She dredged through her memory, but all she could remember was Carlos stepping into the shower, his curt admission that Simon had escaped their net...and the incredible moments of slippery, slithery passion that followed.

"No."

Long silence followed. Marcus stared at her from behind the screen of those damned glasses.

"Margarita, I—"

"Hola!"

The shout spun Marcus around. Margarita side-stepped and saw a squat youngster of four or five charging down the beach.

"Ramon, Señorita! He's coming!"

Squinting, she searched the undulating waves. "There, that must be Ramon's boat. Let's go."

They arrived in San Rico an hour later, jubilation pulsing in their veins. Ramon, bless his keen fisherman's recall, had remembered the registry number of the boat he'd taken Simon and his companion to.

Tires squealing on the cobblestones, Marcus wheeled onto the street that led past San Rico's main square. When the elaborate stone facade of the Ministry of Defense came into view, Margarita screeched a command.

"Stop here! We can go up to Carlos's office and use his secure phone. It's closer."

"Good thinking."

Whipping into a no-parking zone, Marcus shoved the BMW into park and yanked the keys from the ignition. He followed a few steps behind Margarita as she dashed through the corridors and up the stairs to the second floor. As deputy minister of defense, Carlos occupied a corner suite of offices that looked over the square. She'd visited him on several occasions. Enough to confidently wave aside the efficient administrative assistant who jumped to her feet when Margarita and Marcus hurried past.

"Is he in?"

"Yes, but he's got someone with him in his office."

"That's all right. I don't think he'll mind the interruption. Not with the news we've got for him."

"Señorita de las Fuentes! Let me ring him."

The secretary reached for the phone at the same time Margarita twisted the brass knob. She pushed the heavy oak-paneled door open and stumbled to a halt.

Carlos had someone with him in his office, all right, and she was wrapped around him like sticky flypaper.

Chapter 14

Margarita needed only one glance at Carlos's exasperated expression to tell her exactly what had happened.

Anna, sweet, viperish little Anna, had taken advantage of her cousin's long drive to the fishing village to follow through on her threat. She'd obviously tried very hard to make Carlos want her.

Fury surged hot and fast through Margarita's veins. Stalking across the sun-drenched office, she hissed a warning. "You'd better have your hands off him by the time I reach you."

Her cousin's tear-drenched eyes rounded to saucers. With a little squeal, she untangled her arms and darted behind Carlos's broad back. Satisfied that Anna had gotten the message, Margarita planted both hands on her hips and tipped him a narrow-eyed glare.

"I know we said we'd work something out between us. Just so you know, that something isn't going to include cuddling my twit of a cousin every time she runs to you to sob out her problems."

An arrested expression jumped into his eyes. "How do you know that's what happened?"

"Because I know Anna." Some of the belligerence faded from her face. "And I know you. As irritating as you are at times, you're not the kind of man to play games with one woman when you... When you..."

"Love another." He supplied with a slow smile.

As quickly as it had flared, her fury died. An answering smile curved her lips. "Yes. Almost as much as she loves you."

His chest pounding at the frank admission, Carlos started toward her. Another squeak and a nervous tug on his coattails stopped him. Or maybe it was the flicker of raw emotion that crossed the face of the man standing behind Margarita. Marcus caught Carlos's glance on him and quickly summoned a sardonic grin.

"If you two are finished with these nauseating

personal testimonials, maybe we could get to the business that brought us here. Can we use your secure phone?''

''Of course.''

Courteous but firm, Carlos escorted a thoroughly embarrassed Anna to the door. She wouldn't look at him when he closed the door gently behind them.

''You should have told me you love Margarita,'' she sniffed.

Diplomatically, he refrained from pointing out that he'd attempted to do exactly that several times, most recently at the ball two weeks ago.

''I thought...'' Tears of mortification rolled down her cheeks. ''I thought...''

''Why don't you find Miguel?'' he suggested gently. ''I think he's downstairs, in the—''

''He's right here.''

The stocky lieutenant marched in from the hall, his expression thunderous. His gaze whipped from Anna's tear-streaked face to his superior's.

''What did you do to her?''

Before Carlos could decide how to answer that without embarrassing Margarita's young cousin even more or inciting Miguel to take a swing at him, Anna sniffed again and tossed back her hair.

''He didn't do anything, much as I begged him to.''

Head high, she stomped past the lieutenant. She passed him at the door and fired a broadside.

"If you'd tried to kiss me even once, Miguel Carreras, instead of worshipping at my feet like a lovesick puppy, maybe I wouldn't have had to beg Carlos for anything."

Thunderstruck, Miguel gaped at his boss for all of a second or two, then swung around and followed her.

"Anna, wait!"

"I'm tired of waiting. Tired of your—umph!"

Carlos shot his secretary an amused glance and sauntered to the door. The sight of his aide bending Anna over his arm while a corridor full of uniformed soldiers grinned and hooted encouragement gratified him intensely.

The sight that greeted him when he strolled into his office a few moments later afforded him considerably less gratification. Marcus had one hip hitched on the edge his desk, the phone plastered to his ear. Margarita paced impatiently in front of him.

"Once we run down this boat registration," Marcus was saying, "we'll get Navy and Air Force assets out to conduct a search. If it's anywhere in the Caribbean, we'll find it. Simon won't get away this time."

"I wish I could be in on the takedown!"

"Not a problem. After what you went through at the bastard's hands, Jonah will certainly agree you need to be there for the kill. But…''

His glance flicked to Carlos, standing very still just inside the door, then to Margarita.

"Are you sure you want to go into field operations? You're doing great work here."

"Desk work," she muttered.

"Well," Marcus said cheerfully. "Here's your chance to get down and dirty. Just say the word, babe."

The indecision on her face knotted Carlos's stomach.

He could do this, he told himself fiercely. He could stand back and watch the woman he loved put her life on the line. She was a trained professional. She'd proved herself more than capable of handling any contingency.

Forcing a calm smile, he strolled forward. "I take it you got a lead on Simon's trail."

"Yes," she answered, eagerness springing into her eyes. "We've got the registration number of the boat that picked him and one of his men up just off the coast of Madrileño two days ago."

"Good work."

"SPEAR is running a trace on the boat and its movements now," Marcus volunteered. "We're holding on while the computers crunch the satellite images for this sector of—'' He broke off and snapped his attention to the phone. ''Yeah, I'm here. What have you got?''

Carlos moved to stand beside Margarita. He could almost feel the excitement radiating from her slender body. He was losing her. At least for the next few weeks or months or however long it took to run this operation. Then he'd have her back with him...until the next time SPEAR called her.

He could do this, he swore fiercely. Dammit, he could do this.

''Hot damn!''

Marcus dropped the phone into its cradle. His blue eyes blazed with excitement.

''We've got him! The cross match of radio signals, navigational beacons and satellite imagery tracked our boy from just off Madrileño's coast. According to their vectors, he's heading for the island of Cascadilla.''

''Cascadilla?'' Margarita grasped the significance of the small Caribbean island instantly. ''Isn't that where SPEAR has some kind of an R and R center?''

''It is. It must be the next target in Simon's personal vendetta against SPEAR.''

Marcus pushed off the desk, ready for action.

''There's a plane in the air as we speak. It'll be at the San Rico airport at approximately twenty-one hundred hours. Next stop, Cascadilla.''

Chapter 15

Heedless of his hand-tailored black tux, Carlos leaned a hip against the stone balustrade and let the soft Madrileñan moonlight wash over him.

The rum-soaked outer wrapping on his glowing cigar sent a curl of fragrant smoke into the air. A buzz of conversation drifted through the row of French doors thrown open to the balmy night, drowning out the string quartet assembled to entertain the guests gathered to meet Argentina's new cultural attaché to Madrileño.

Carlos wouldn't have heard the quartet even without the swell of lively conversation. He'd come out to the flagstone balcony with every sense tuned to the airport clearly visible from the higher elevation of the Presidential Palace.

The airport approach lights glowed red and white in the darkness. Taxiways were outlined in blue. He flicked a glance at his watch. Marcus said the plane would land in San Rico at twenty-one hundred hours. Nine o'clock. Fifteen minutes ago. By now, Margarita and Marcus would have their gear loaded. The plane should be taking off again at any minute.

Carlos had opted not to go to the airport with Margarita. He had to get used to her leaving on short notice. Had to get used to coming home to an empty house.

Rolling the cigar in his fingers, he tried to convince himself that the hours between her visit to his office this afternoon and her departure tonight would compensate for the empty nights to come. She'd been so loving, so passionate...

"Carlos?"

His head whipped around. With a small crunch, the cigar disintegrated in his fingers. Disbelieving, he stared at the slender figure in the flame-colored gown.

Light spilled through the French doors behind her, glinting on the thick, glossy hair swept up in a smooth twist. Carlos felt his chest constrict. He cleared his throat, but the best he could manage was a gruff sentence, "You look very beautiful in red, my darling."

She glided forward, a smile on her lips. "So you've told me."

Her face was in shadow, but moonlight gleamed on the smooth line of her throat and shoulders.

Her *bare* throat and shoulders.

It took a second for his stunned mind to register the absence of the gold locket she always wore. The vise around his chest tightened another notch.

"I thought you were leaving with Marcus."

"I thought I was, too. I got as far as the airport."

"What changed your mind?"

"Knowing you accepted that I could leave at any time suddenly made leaving not nearly as important as staying. Does that make sense?"

"Perfect sense," he growled.

Tossing the remains of his cigar over the stone railing, he opened his arms. Margarita filled them, just as she filled his heart.

Carlos crushed her to him. Her mouth found his, eager, joyful, hungry. He didn't think he could love her more than he did at that moment, but when she drew back, her eyes alight with the special glow that was hers alone, he realized he was wrong. He'd love her a little more with every breath he drew.

"You'd better marry me," she told him. "My

mother assures me that no one will think anything about us living together in this day and age, *but…*''

"A wise woman, your mother."

"Very wise." She searched his face. "She also suggested I run for that vacant Senate seat, if you don't want it."

"You're welcome to it."

"You don't mind? Honestly?"

"I would be proud."

He grinned at her, guessing what was coming next. She didn't disappoint him.

"And when my uncle's term is up, I may just consider running for President."

"You'd make an excellent head of state." The laughter faded from his voice. "There's much to do here in Madrileño. We could do it together."

"That's one of the reasons I didn't get on the plane. A small part."

"And the other reasons?"

"There's only one."

Sliding her palm up the black satin lapels, she rose on tiptoe to brush his mouth with hers once again.

"You, *mi amor.* You."

* * * * *

Next month, don't miss
Merline Lovelace's incredible
MIRA Books debut—
THE HORSE SOLDIER.
This passionate historical romance
is on sale in February 2001.

And coming soon to
Intimate Moments, look for
TWICE IN ONE LIFETIME,
part of Merline's gripping
MEN OF THE BAR H series,
on sale in April 2001.

And now, here's a sneak preview of
SOMEONE TO WATCH OVER HER
by Margaret Watson,
the next riveting book in
A YEAR OF LOVING DANGEROUSLY,
available next month!

Chapter 1

Marcus Waters kicked at a shell on the sand and watched it somersault into the frothy blue waters of the Caribbean. It reminded him of his heart, he thought sourly, tumbled and tossed by his futile passion for Margarita Alfonsa de las Fuentes.

It was just as well, he told himself as he continued walking down the deserted beach, that Margarita had chosen Carlos Caballero. He wasn't interested in a long-term relationship, except for the ones that ended with a goodbye kiss in the morning. Margarita and Carlos belonged together. And he belonged by himself. He'd learned that years ago.

244 Someone To Watch Over Her

He pulled the loneliness around him like a cloak, using it to harden his heart and seal it against any more painful blows. He had his job, and that was all that mattered. That was all he wanted.

And right now, his job was to spend time on this beautiful tropical island, waiting for the elusive Simon to show up. Simon had been attacking the SPEAR agency for several months, trying to destroy what had taken over a century to build.

Marcus was just one of a dozen agents dedicated to catching Simon and stopping his ruthless campaign. And their intelligence had told them that Simon was headed here to Cascadilla.

As he walked along the beach, he noticed the gulls and other shorebirds screeching and diving toward a dark bundle on the sand. He walked a little faster. After years as an agent, he paid attention to everything. His life could depend on knowing the details.

There were pale tentacles on the bundle, and he frowned as he walked a little faster. The hairs on the back of his neck stood up, and suddenly he broke into a run. That was no bundle of seaweed. That was a body, lying half in the water and half on the sand.

He dropped to his knees next to the body, which was facedown in the sand. It was a woman. Her wet reddish-blond hair was tangled and matted with sand and salt. Marcus reached for her neck and felt a pulse, thready but present. Reassured that she was alive, he ran his hands over her quickly, looking for broken bones. Finding nothing, he gently turned her onto her back.

He watched the rise and fall of her chest for a moment, reassured that it was regular and even, then put his ear against her ribs and listened to her breathe. Her lungs were clear, which meant that she hadn't almost drowned.

Marcus rocked on his heels and stared at the unknown woman. She looked very young, and although she was bedraggled and bruised, he could see that she was beautiful.

What had happened to her? How had she ended up on this deserted part of the beach, unconscious and alone?

He couldn't leave her lying in the sand. Scooping her into his arms, he headed to his beachfront cottage at the Westwind Falls Resort.

Her body felt chilled in his arms, and in order to keep her warm he shifted her so that most of her body was pressed against his. The weight of her breasts flattened against his chest, and her nipples burned into his skin through the thin, wet material of her shirt. Her thigh brushed against his groin, electrifying him.

His hands tightened on her firm, smooth skin, and instinctively he pulled her closer. His body stirred, shifting and adjusting to touch more of her.

Shocked at his unexpected response, he adjusted her in his arms so that she wasn't pressed so intimately against him. But she groaned softly and moved restlessly against him, and once again they were touching as intimately as lovers.

The lights of the resort twinkled through the gathering darkness, and he exhaled with relief. The sooner he got this woman to his cottage and called an ambulance, the happier he would be. His reaction to her closeness was unsettling and disturbing.

His cottage stood slightly apart from the others, the last in the row before the development surrendered to the beach and the dense tropical foliage that began at the edge of the sand. Since Westwood Falls Resort was owned by SPEAR, this cottage was always available for an agent who needed it.

Entering the cottage, he laid the woman in his arms gently on the bed in the large bedroom, then took a step back and looked at her.

She looked small and fragile and vulnerable lying on the huge bed. She needed to get to a hospital. He picked up the phone that stood on the nightstand next to the bed and began to dial the local emergency number. But before he finished dialing, the woman cried out.

"No!" The single word reverberated with panic. "No, don't."

Quickly he set the telephone receiver into its cradle and knelt next to the bed. "It's all right," he said in a low voice. "No one's going to hurt you."

Her eyes remained closed, but her hands clenched into fists on the bedspread. "Stay away from me! Get out!"

He reached for her hand and cupped her tight fist between his palms. Her hands were small and delicate, the bones tiny and fragile. "Relax," he murmured. "You're safe now."

What had happened to her? He stood up slowly, his gut churning with anxiety as he stared at her. Whatever had happened to this woman was more than an accident. Someone had deliberately tried to hurt her. And judging from where and how he had found her, she was probably still in danger.

She cried out again, and he sat on the bed with her. "You're safe now," he repeated, speaking in a low, soothing voice. He continued to reassure her until she stopped moving around on the bed.

Somewhere, someone was looking for this woman. Someone who meant her harm. The familiar adrenaline of a case rose inside him, making his heart pound, sharpening his senses. No one would hurt her, he vowed. He would make sure of that!